MYSTERY AT MOVIE MANOR

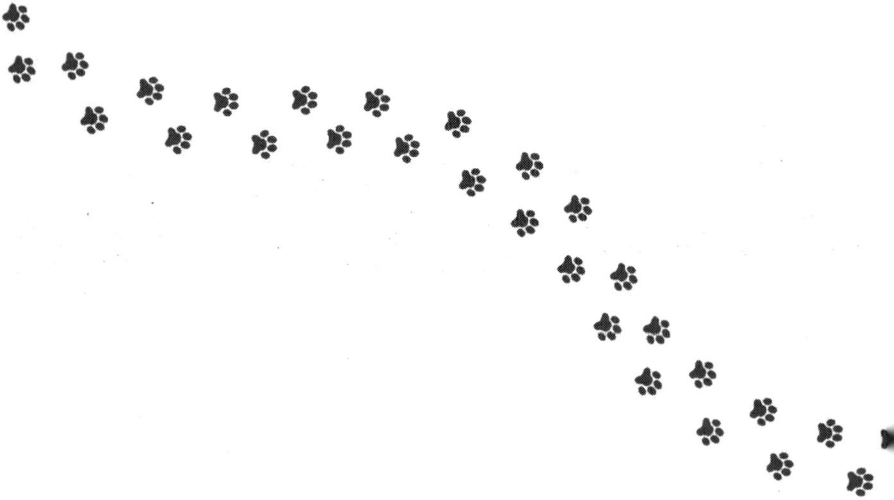

MYSTERY AT MOVIE MANOR

STUART MCPHERSON

Matador
Unit E2 Airfield Business Park,
Harrison Road, Market Harborough,
Leicestershire. LE16 7UL
Tel: 0116 2792299
Email: books@troubador.co.uk
Web: www.troubador.co.uk/matador
Twitter: @matadorbooks

ISBN 978 1805140 221

British Library Cataloguing in Publication Data.
A catalogue record for this book is available from the British Library.

Printed and bound in Great Britain by 4edge Limited
Typeset in 12pt Baskerville by Troubador Publishing Ltd, Leicester, UK

Matador is an imprint of Troubador Publishing Ltd

To my mother and father

ACKNOWLEDGEMENTS

First and foremost to Raj Bhaskar who got me started really trying to write (though in my slow-witted way it took me many years to produce this). Thanks also to him for permission to give one of my characters his forename. Thanks too to David Pettigrew and Cathy McSporran and my fellow students in the writing classes they ran for the advice and encouragement they all gave me.

ONE

PLAYING THE ELF PRINCE

A fair-haired boy and girl crouched behind a boulder. Beyond them was a huge screen which glowed with a deep blue colour. A young elf boy swung through the air and landed beside them. He moved awkwardly for a wire was attached to his back, connecting him to an overhead crane. He pointed the white staff in his hand.

"Biodh solas mor ann!" he cried, thrusting his staff towards the screen. It glowed as he pressed a button.

1

The children stood staring at the blue screen for several seconds, while a camera moved in close to them. A voice suddenly roared out.

"Cut! Well done, kids. That's a wrap everybody."

The children visibly relaxed. The blond children glared at each other.

"You make a really ugly boy, Carol," said her sister, Melody.

"Huh!" Carol stuck her tongue out. "You make an even uglier girl."

"How can you talk like that to each other?" The elf boy was puzzled. "You're twins – you look exactly like each other."

The girls laughed. Then they hugged.

"It's just our way of letting off steam," said Carol. "We always have nerves during filming."

"You're the opposite, Iain," said Melody. "You're really nervous until we start filming and then you're as cool as bucket of ice."

A big, rather fat, bearded man in a bright red T-shirt plodded over. This was Oswald Wales, the director and scriptwriter of the movie which was being filmed for television.

"That was just great, kids. No need for any more retakes. You can have the rest of the day off."

The children groaned.

"It's nearly seven o'clock," Carol told him. "We should have finished ages ago."

"Almost dinner time then. You'd better go and get something to eat. Don't forget to go over your lines for tomorrow. One more big scene and a few short scenes then you'll have plenty of spare time."

Iain moved to leave with the girls but was jerked back by the wire attached to him. The twins tried not to laugh – but failed and doubled up with mirth.

"… Dot! Come and help Iain here!"

Dorothy ('Dot'), who organised the stunts involving the children, came running over.

"Hold still! I need to unfasten your jacket before I can get the line off."

The 'line' was a thin, strong wire that held Iain suspended so that he 'flew' into the scene.

Carol and Melody came over to watch.

"It must be fun to fly," said Melody, wistfully. "Why is the wire painted blue?"

"It's so they can make it invisible." Carol was scornful. "It's the same as the blue screen we've been using today in the Barn."

The Barn belonged to the Laird who owned the land they were filming on, in the Scottish Highlands. The film crew had rebuilt it inside as a miniature studio. Later, when it was edited, images could be added in place of the blue screen: weird landscapes or monsters or other effects. Their story was a fantasy involving wizards and elves… and three children who were feeling very hungry.

Iain was freed from the wire now but was

struggling with the harness underneath his jacket.

"Keep still!" said Dot. "Ouch!"

"Look," Iain told the twins, "you go ahead, and I'll catch you up."

"Oh yes," said Melody, "you're staying over at the Hall tonight, aren't you? I forgot."

"Silly!" Carol tugged her sister's pigtails. This didn't bother her a bit since it was a wig which came away in her hand, showing Melody's own hair, cut short like her twin's. The crew laughed and even Iain, who was always rather serious, smiled. Dot looked up and shooed them off.

"You lot get yourselves changed and cleaned before dinner. Go on!"

They trotted off, leaving Iain in the Barn with Dot and the crew members who were tidying up and putting gear away for the night. With no distractions now, he quickly got the harness off. Dot slapped his shoulder to let him know he could go.

"Hurry and get changed – and don't forget your ears!"

Iain clapped his hands to the side of his face. He could feel the sharp tips glued to the tops of his ears, which gave him his elf look. They were made of a special, soft plastic material so that he hardly noticed he had them on.

"Oh!"

In the dresser's caravan Carol and Melody were just getting into their normal clothes. Rosie was hanging up their costumes and Liz was tidying Melody's wig.

"Ears!" she shouted and pointed to the corner where there was a chair, a mirror and boxes of makeup.

The other children laughed. She always shouted this when she saw Iain. He sat down while Liz applied a solvent to the tips of his ears. While he waited for it to act, he pulled off his elf boots and velvet trews. Soon his elf ears were off and stored and Rosie put away his costume while he put on his everyday clothes. He had just pulled on his jeans when Carol told him to hurry up.

"Nearly ready!" he mumbled from beneath the sweater he was dragging on. Then they jumped on their bikes and were off. A minibus and a couple of Landrovers usually ran the actors to and from wherever they were filming. The children preferred to make the journey on their bikes – unless it rained. None of the locations they had used so far were more than a few miles from the Hall and they could get around pretty quickly in the quiet country lanes. Iain came by bike whatever the weather, for unlike the others, he did not normally stay at the famous old estate of the Laird of Clairaig. Also, unlike the others, he was a local boy, from the nearby village of Laganglas. He had not even been one of the actors until after the filming had started. He had been 'discovered' as the old expression said, standing in a crowd of other children from the village watching the filming. Oswald had spotted him and, believing he could replace a boy actor who had been injured, signed him to appear in the picture.

Iain was joining his new friends to sleep over at the Laird's manor. Apart from the room where they rehearsed, he had never actually seen the inside of the place. Carol called over her shoulder to him.

"You promised you'd show us the glen. We'll have plenty of time to do that now. I want to see the wildlife up there."

"It's hard to believe it's nearly all over," said Iain. "The time has just flown by."

"We've still got some scenes to do so we'll have to work some days." Carol made a face. "I bet Oswald thinks of extra stuff for us to do. He's always changing the script. I was a girl at the start and he changed me to a boy."

Iain laughed at this, though he knew what she meant. Soon they were cycling through the north gate and along the driveway towards the main entrance.

It was an amazing place, as fantastical as anything in the fantasy story they were filming. It was shining white and looked, in the soft evening light, just like a fairy palace. Clairaig Hall it was called, yet that seemed too ordinary for such a wonderful place. The children called it the Elves' Palace, though local folk had taken to calling it Movie Manor because of the film people staying there. Some of the rooms inside it were as fantastic as the building itself. It was a place that made you feel magic was real and amazing, unbelievable things could really happen. Which was probably why they weren't surprised when a lion suddenly roared at them.

It clattered against the high chain fence that ran alongside the driveway. The fence ran for several miles, enclosing an area near the manor that was a kind of 'open-air' zoo or 'safari park'. Because the driveway ran a long and circuitous route towards the manor it passed close by the park fence at this point. Within the zoo area various kinds of animal lived together – except the predators, who were kept in their own fenced-off areas within the main park so they wouldn't eat all the other animals.

"Wow," said Carol, "what's up with old Leo. He's in a bad temper today."

"Maybe he's got toothache," said Melody. "Hey! Imagine having to pull out one of these teeth."

"And he's got bad breath too," added Iain. "Hey! Stop following us!"

The lion, attracted by their swift motion, was running alongside them. Iain stared at it, wonderingly, for he had never been up to see the zoo before. It was a relatively recent tourist attraction and was expensive. Soon however the driveway curved away from the fence and the lion disappeared from view.

Some minutes later the manor itself hove into view. Dinner and a well-earned rest were waiting them… or so they thought.

The children were huddled round the great fireplace in Lady Mary's Room. It was a comfortable place with a great fur rug and plenty of cushions to lie about on. The room was small, and it had a rather dark, claustrophobic atmosphere. It was an old room, filled with dark and very solid, ancient furniture.

"A good place for ghosts," said Iain when he saw it for the first time.

"Don't say that!" said Melody, horrified.

Carol laughed.

"Jamie, the caretaker here, told us this place is haunted by the Laird's great-great grandmother. Apparently, she committed suicide – threw herself off the old tower. But I suppose he made that up."

The old tower was part of the original castle, which had stood on the site of the manor in the Middle Ages. Later it had been rebuilt and turned into the palatial building that everybody now knew. Some old parts of the original castle still remained, however, including the old tower. That was usually kept locked as there were no living spaces in it, being mostly used for storage.

"It does look sinister," Melody had said, "just the place for ghosts and ghouls. Although probably it's only full of old junk and cobwebs."

"I suppose," said Carol, yawning, "we'd better go over tomorrow's script."

They got their scripts out and found comfortable places to sit or sprawl.

"It's funny seeing you two play different genders," said Iain. "You usually play identical twins. Mind, I've seen you both play the same character."

"We do that quite often," said Carol, laughing. "Children can't work the same hours as adult actors, but if they use twins for the same part, they can swap them round so they get more filming done with them."

"Hey!" Melody shook her head. "Look – this script has been changed again. That Oswald Wales and his rewrites!"

"Yes," said Iain. "He keeps putting me in new scenes."

"Didn't you notice before?" Melody said. "He really likes you as the elf prince, so he's building up your part."

"That's right," said Carol in a sarcastic tone, "you're a big star now!"

"I am not!" Iain's cheeks were burning. "My part's not as big as yours."

The twins laughed at his embarrassment.

"Who knows?" said Carol. "It might lead to other acting parts for you."

"Let's get on with the script," said Melody. "Once we finish this scene tomorrow, we'll have a good break and you can take us to the glen."

"It will probably be pouring by then," said Carol with a groan. "We've had such terrific weather since we started filming."

"Yes," said Iain. "Oswald's had his second unit out filming all sorts of scenery to use later. They were up at the glen today, filming at the old broch."

"What on earth is a bro*ck*?" asked Carol, not quite catching Iain's pronunciation.

"Ha-ha!" said Melody, making a sarcastic, not-quite-really-a-laugh noise. "Don't you know anything?"

"Well, super-brain, what is it then?"

"It's a kind of old tower that people lived in long ago. A sort of castle but all round instead of square."

"The ancient Celts built them long ago," said Iain. "You know, it's a funny thing but the old broch is supposed to be haunted too."

"Never!" said Melody. "We're supposed to be filming a big scene there."

"If we do," said Carol, "it will be in bright daylight, so you needn't be afraid of a ghost."

Melody smacked her script copy on her sister's head.

"Let's get on with this."

"All right."

They all sat up, gathering round closer. Carol, as the oldest (by fifteen minutes), took the lead.

"Right, there are only two adults in our scenes. I'll read the wizard's lines and Melody can do the old hag (*ha-ha*). You just do your own lines, Iain."

Carol cleared her throat and spoke in a rather deep voice, trying to sound like an adult.

"What do ye in my woods, strangers? None may enter unless they give me what they hold most dear! Ha-ha-ha-ha-ha-hah!"

"For heaven's sake, we don't need that," said Iain.

"I hope Martin doesn't ham it up like that tomorrow," said Melody. "What a cackle!"

"Come on, I'm just trying to give an impression of the thing. It's your line anyway."

"All right," said Melody, "ahem! *Oh sir, we lost our way in the storm and were looking for shelter.*"

"No matter! You have trespassed so you must pay the penalty... Run for it!"

Carol did the last phrase in her normal voice as that was her part, as the boy, Billy. Then she said: "Now all the wolf-men come creeping out from the dark and surround us. Then it's your line, Iain."

Iain raised his arm, a pencil standing in for the elf prince's magic staff. *"By this power of light, I charge you, be gone! Air Falbh!"*

"They're still coming!" cried Melody, as loud and as scared as if she really was out in the woods surrounded by horrible creatures.

"Your feeble magic can do nothing in my domain, elf-brat!" said Carol in her wizard voice.

"Look!" said Melody, pointing, *"there's a gap there."*

"Then we all run towards the stream with the wolf-men howling away like anything. That takes us on to the next scene. We've escaped and we stagger inside the tower – which will actually be the brock…"

"*Broch*!" said Iain, very loudly. "A brock is a badger, not a tower."

"Will you stop going on about that? Anyway, we'll do the interior scene in the Barn studio. They've built a nice, gloomy dungeon. Pay attention! When we try to get some sleep, we're woken up by a horrible…"

And just then there was the most horrible screech.

TWO

GHOST IN THE TOWER

The children jumped to their feet. The terrible sound fitted in so well with the ghostly scene they had all been imagining that for one moment they thought it must really be a ghost.

"It can't be," said Iain. "Someone's playing a trick on us."

He ran to the door and pulled it open quickly. But no one was there.

"I think it sounded like it came from upstairs somewhere," said Melody.

They all looked at each other. The nearest stairs led up inside the old tower and nobody ever went there.

"It can't be the tower, it must be the floor above us," said Carol, looking up.

Iain walked to the door that opened into the passage to the tower.

"Oh, no… don't!" gasped Melody as he opened it.

"Don't be silly," said Carol. "It's just somebody mucking around… Oh!"

The screech sounded again. With the passage door open they could tell for sure now that it came from the tower. Iain ran to the end of the short passage and grabbed the handle of the door to the tower staircase. But it was locked.

"Then it must really be a ghost!" cried Melody. "No one can be up there if the door's locked. Let's get away from here."

"Don't be silly," Carol told her. "Iain's right; it must be a trick. Someone's playing a stupid joke."

"But the door…"

"It could be locked from the inside," said Iain. "Shall we get the caretaker now and tell him what happened?"

"Let's not tell anyone who's in charge," said Carol. "If it was just a prank, we don't want to get whoever it is into trouble. They might lose their job."

"If it was a prank!" said Melody. "Huh! I think it was a nasty trick, scaring us like that."

"Still, Carol has a point," said Iain. "I wouldn't like to get anyone fired. Look, is there any other way into the tower?"

"I don't think so," said Melody. "*Wait a minute!* Old Cromarty would know. He does odd jobs here and I saw him trimming a hedge earlier. We could ask him."

"And he might have a key," said Carol. "We could get him to open the door and find out who's been playing tricks on us."

"I know him," said Iain. "I'm sure if we asked, he'd keep it to himself."

So, they ran outside and round to the side of the manor where they found Old Cromarty. He was sitting on an upturned box, wiping his brow and smoking a pipe. Although it was evening it was still very warm. Iain greeted him in Gaelic.

"Ciamar a tha sibh?" *How are you?*

The old man smiled, recognising Iain.

"Chan eil dona. Ciamar a tha thu fhein?" *Not bad. How art thou, thyself?[1]*

---

1   Gaelic you is like French (with vous and tu). Iain addresses Cromarty who is adult with formal sibh. Cromarty uses informal thu because he is talking to a child.

15

"I'm fine, thank you," replied Iain, switching back to ordinary English. "It's nice speaking Gaelic to someone, but Carol and Melody don't understand so it would be rude to go on."

"Aye. But didn't I hear you using some Gaelic when you were doing your film acting the other day?"

"Oh!" said Melody. "Oswald told him to do that. He doesn't understand it any more than we do but he likes the sound of it. So do I."

"Yes, he told me to throw in the odd Gaelic phrase. It's supposed to be the language elves speak."

Cromarty laughed and had to grab his pipe to stop it falling from his mouth.

"If there were such things as elves, I am sure Gaelic is what they would speak. But this is all by the by. What is it that you want?"

They quickly told him what had happened. The old man looked at them suspiciously, his grey eyes peering into theirs. He had a strangely intense stare which made them feel as if he was looking into their hearts to see if they were telling the truth. At last, he decided.

"All right. Let us see what you have discovered. No one ought to be in the old tower… no one human. But… well, I suppose ghosts are not too bad while it's yet daylight."

The children were not sure if Cromarty was serious. Did he believe it was a ghost? Perhaps he was only joking. Inside, Cromarty pulled a long chain from his pocket which held a ring of keys. There were candlesticks standing on the cupboards and Iain grabbed a couple of them.

"It's bound to be dark in the tower."

They found matches in the cupboard drawer and lit the candles. Cromarty unlocked the door. It was stiff and only opened with a really hard pull – and a really horrible creak.

Iain entered first. Carol followed, with Melody close behind. Old Cromarty merely stood, puffing at his pipe, a faint smile on his wrinkled face. There was a terrific clatter.

"Careful, Iain!" said Carol. "You'll have all this rubbish falling down on us."

And the stairwell was certainly cluttered with bits of old furniture, boxes and old papers. The children had to push their way through all the rubbish to make their way up the stairs.

"You know," said Iain, "I don't think anyone could have come this way. They'd have knocked everything over."

"It's all a mess though," said Carol, "they might just have shoved everything aside."

"Yes, but then there'd be marks in the dust – look at the ground."

"The children looked down. Behind them and all the way up to where Iain was standing their footmarks could be clearly seen on the dusty steps. But beyond him, higher up the stairs, the dust lay undisturbed.

No one had been up these stairs for ages! Melody was bewildered.

"But someone must have come up the stairs!" she said. "We heard them…" Her voice trailed off. She looked at the others for support.

"Well," said Iain, "it sounded like it came from up there, but I suppose—"

"It definitely did come from there," said Carol. "Maybe there's another way up?"

"Not that I ever heard of," said Cromarty, and he sucked at his pipe, which had just gone out. He struck a match. "Perhaps there *is* a way in – for a ghost! After all, walls won't stop a ghost, or so I've heard."

He got his pipe lit and gave it a few puffs while gesturing at the children to come back down the stairs.

"I'd best lock this again," he told them. "Maybe you just imagined…"

And at that moment there was another awful screech from somewhere above them – somewhere in the tower! Iain ran up the stairs and disappeared round the corner. The others stood, shocked and frozen to the spot; then they too ran up after him.

Carol and Melody piled into the back of Iain and they all nearly went down in a heap. The stairs had ended suddenly and unexpectedly, and they'd all gone barging through an unlocked door and out onto the parapet at the top of the tower. For a moment they were blinded as the low, evening sun shone into their eyes and they weren't sure exactly what had happened. Then they saw the green fields of the manor grounds and the nearby woods and hills beyond. At their backs was the door opening from the turret roof onto its surrounding parapet. Suddenly there was another loud screech. Melody screamed and even Iain, who had been quite reckless, jumped a little.

"It came from the other side, I think," said Carol, a little nervously.

They looked at one another. If one of them then had suggested they go back down again, they all probably would have. But each one was afraid to let on to the others that they were scared so they stayed, glancing nervously around. Then Carol began to walk round the parapet. The others followed close behind. None of them wanted to be left alone to meet whatever it was that was hiding up on top of the tower. If they had to meet something – or some *thing* – whatever it was, they would much rather meet it together. They went round slowly, all the time half expecting something to suddenly jump out at them. Round they went, to the other side where they could look down on the roof of the main building, but nothing was there, so they kept going. At last, they were back where they started, standing in the bright sunlight once more.

"Well, here's the door again," said Carol. "I don't understand it. There doesn't seem to be anything up here after all."

Iain was not so sure. "This turret thing is quite wide. Someone could have walked quietly along in front of us and we'd never have seen them."

"Let's split up," suggested Carol. "You go that way Iain and—"

"Oh, no!" said Melody. "I think we'd better stick together. We don't know what's up here." She looked around nervously.

"Don't be so soft!" said Carol.

This annoyed Melody: she felt half embarrassed and half angry. She always believed she was as brave as her sister – though at the moment she didn't believe it very strongly. They began to argue with each other – perhaps because they were all scared. Soon, their voices were raised so loud that they could be heard by Old Cromarty, still standing at the bottom of the stairs. It might have developed into a terrible row except they were interrupted by another horrible screech. They all stood frozen and suddenly wordless. There was a sudden scrabbling and scraping sound followed by a tremendous thump. Then there was another awful screech. This time however they could tell where it was coming from: they looked up and there, on the circular roof above them, was a great hairy ape. The noise they had made must have upset it for it was jumping up and down screeching and banging on the rooftop. Carol laughed.

"Paint me green and call me a pickle! There's your ghost," she said. "It's just a big monkey."

"That's an ape," Melody told her. "It must have escaped from the zoo park."

"We'd better get away from here," said Iain. "I think it's scared. Frightened animals can turn nasty."

Iain was about to say that they should not make any sudden movements when the ape screeched again and leaped from the roof. It flew over the heads of the children and landed on the parapet wall. Then it struck Iain a blow that knocked him sideways against the turret wall. Although it was not much bigger than the children, it was wild and strong. It bared fierce-looking teeth, with huge, sharp incisors. Carol and Melody helped Iain to his feet.

"Move slowly," said Carol, speaking in a quiet voice so not to upset the creature. "Once we're through the door we can lock it out."

They slid very gradually along the wall and up to the doorway – they could do little else anyway for Iain was rather stunned and the girls had to guide him along between them. All the time the ape glared at them ferociously and they were sure that at any moment it would leap at them and bite them. Then, just as they thought they were about to make it safely in through the doorway, it suddenly gathered itself, ready to attack them.

THREE

THE WILD ONES?

At that very moment several flashing white shapes flew down, flapping and squealing around the tower – seagulls! The manor was only a few miles from the sea, hidden from view by the westerly hills. Silly, foolish birds they were but they saved the children. The ape jumped up and down on the parapet, screaming again; but now all of its anger was directed at the birds. As the children moved into the safety

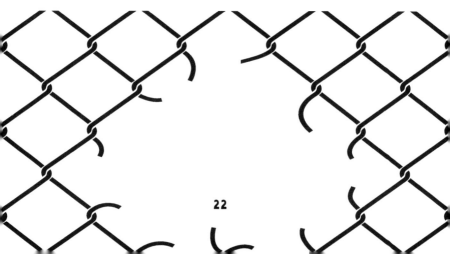

of the doorway, the ape leapt – but over and above them onto the roof, chasing the screeching seabirds. What a racket they all made! The children clattered downstairs as fast as they could. Moments later, they burst out of the tower and into the hall at the bottom of the stairs. Old Cromarty was still standing there and seemed not the least bothered by their frightened faces or that they were all shouting at the top of their voices.

"So," he said, with an infuriating grin, "you will have seen your ghost then?"

The children had calmed down a little and got some breath back, so they managed to gabble out what had happened.

Cromarty calmly pushed the children to one side and locked the door.

"That thing up there probably climbed up the wall but there's no sense letting it into the house. Hmmm… I wonder how it got out o' the park."

Old Cromarty was somewhat stiff in his legs even at the best of times. All this excitement after a busy day's work had left him feeling quite done in. He settled himself into a nearby seat.

"Don't worry, Old Crom," said Carol. "We'll tell the Laird what happened. Maybe we'll find out how that ape got free."

"I doubt you'll get to talk to the Laird – he's aye busy about this time making sure everything's been tidied up after all the tourists have left."

"We'll find someone to tell anyway," said Iain. "We can't have a wild ape running around free."

"Not to mention, lions and tigers and bears," said Carol.

"Oh, my!" said Melody, giggling.

Iain groaned at this – whether from the old joke or the pain of the ape's blow, it was hard to say. Then he pushed past everyone, saying,

"Let's find someone, anyone, and tell them what happened."

They set off and walked round the manor. As they turned the first corner, they met Ronnie, one of the actresses in their film. She was a good friend and had been especially encouraging to Iain. Ronnie was Veronica Mere, famous as the Victorian lady detective in *Lady Molly of Scotland Yard*. Now she was playing the mother of Melody and Carol's characters. She was always telling them,

"I'm so glad I can speak in my own voice in this picture, and not that terribly posh accent I have to use in *Lady Molly*."

She had a pleasant north England accent, coming originally from a village in Westmorland. After a quick *Hello*, she asked,

"Have any of you seen Harry?"

"Harry?" Iain was puzzled and his friends looked a little surprised.

"Harry Puddock, one of the costumers. His speciality is personal effects – you know, jewellery and other things actors will wear, like bracelets, rings and even crowns. He's an expert jeweller and I'd asked him to repair my necklace as a favour. He said I could collect it today, but he doesn't seem to be about. What are you lot up to anyway?"

They told her quickly what had happened to them.

"Gosh, you daft kids! You could have been seriously injured. How on earth did it get out?"

"We don't know but we have to find someone who works with the animals," said Melody. "We can't have a big ape running about the place."

"Apart from Oswald," said Carol.

Soon they came round to the south side of the house. From here, they could see the big fence which enclosed the open-air zoo though parts were hidden by bushes and trees. Two men were hurrying towards them.

"That looks like Jimmy Cullen and Paul MacDonald," said Ronnie. "They work for the zoo and they don't look pleased. I bet they've seen where your ape got out."

And so they had; and they were angry; and even angrier when they heard what had happened to the children.

"There were holes cut in the fence," said Jimmy.

"Luckily, none of them big enough for one of the lions to get out, but that ape could have hurt someone."

"Yes," said Iain, "me!"

"Well, it looks like a couple of smaller animals got out too – a pair of capybaras – Jock and Sandy will catch them."

"They're pretty harmless," said Paul, "but that's not the point. These animals are valuable and besides something dangerous *could* have got out."

"We'd better get a net and get after that ape," said Jimmy. "Let's hope it's still up in that tower or we'll have to get all the park staff out to catch it."

The children were eager to come along and see the ape being caught but the animal handlers were adamant. They thought it might still be dangerous. They were rather gloomy as they went back to Lady Mary's room.

Back in the manor, they went over their lines again and then went to have a bit of supper. They took their meals into the little side room which was more comfortable than the big dining room. They had just finished when they heard a loud voice in an adjoining room.

"These blasted wild-folk terrorists!"

The voice, roaring as loudly as one of his lions, belonged to Sir Ronald MacKay, the Laird of Clairaig. Indeed, he looked quite like a lion with his broad shoulders, great bushy eyebrows and mane of thick white hair. Loud as he was, they couldn't make out much of what he was saying. All they could tell was that it was about the escaped animals.

"What does he mean, *wild-folk terrorists*?" asked Melody.

"He must mean the *Wildlife Freedom Fighters*," Iain told her. "They call themselves the WFF. Some of them break into labs and release animals being experimented on."

"I know who the WFF are," said Melody. "I just didn't realise Sir Ronald meant them."

"In fact," said Carol, "our mum's a member of the WFF. She doesn't do anything, though; she just gives them donations. I never thought they were bad people."

"They're not," said Iain. "We've got a small group of them up here. They don't do the things that get into the news. They just keep a watch on the wildlife, looking out for poachers who want to steal rare birds or their eggs."

"Why would they do that?" asked Melody.

"Jumping giraffes! Don't you know anything, Mel?" said Carol.

Melody swung a foot at her sister but missed. Iain went on,

"Some rare types of bird are dying out but they're trying to save them. Only the thing is, because they *are* rare, they're worth lots of money to collectors. So there are always crooks trying to steal them and sell them abroad."

"Yes... but why would these people want to release Sir Ronald's animals?" asked Melody. "He doesn't mistreat his animals, does he?"

"Of course not," said Iain, "they're very well treated. They're separated of course so the lions, for instance, don't eat all the deer…"

"… And the lions don't eat the people like us!" Carol laughed at her own joke but none of the others did. They nearly *had* been eaten – or at least badly bitten by that fierce ape.

"Quite a few animals escaped," said Iain. "Luckily only that pair of capybaras wandered very far."

"What on earth is a capybara?" asked Melody. "I was too upset last time to ask."

Iain made gestures with his hands and tried to describe one. Then he got out a pencil and paper and drew a picture.

"That looks a bit like an overgrown hamster with long legs."

"They're about the size of a dog but they're not fierce; however, they *could* have been hurt or even killed."

"Whoever did it must be mad!" said Melody. "They should be locked up."

"QUITE RIGHT, MY DEAR," said a familiar, and very loud, voice from the door. It was Sir Ronald. His face was still flushed with anger. "I'd put the lot of them in with the lions and see how *they'd* feel being attacked by wild animals!"

"You wouldn't really put them in with the lions?" said Iain.

"Why not? The lions nearly got out. Luckily,

they didn't manage to cut a hole big enough for a lion."

"Have you called the police?" asked Carol, hoping there might be more excitement to come.

"Certainly. We found a WFF badge next to a cut in the fence. I've told them to arrest the lot of them."

Iain was horrified.

"You don't mean they'll arrest the local WFF people? None of them could have anything to do with it."

Sir Ronald's eyes flared for a moment but he kept his temper and even smiled at Iain. Unlike some of the people who owned estates in the Highlands, he cared about the local community. He worked closely with the locals and had worked hard to encourage a TV company to come up to Clairaig to make the movie. It meant jobs and good publicity for the area. Sir Ronald had been especially pleased that a local boy like Iain had got a part in the film. Because of this, he found it difficult to remain angry with him.

"Well, maybe it was outsiders – perhaps from the loony wing of their organisation – and not our local lads. I'd like to think so, but I'm sure they can give the police some information. They're all part of the same mob, aren't they?" He cleared his throat loudly, a great *harrumph*! "Well, anyway, I came in to say that since you've had a bit of a fright, you can have a break tomorrow. Oswald has rearranged the shooting schedule so you can have a day off. Iain can show you around."

With that he left, leaving them to wonder what to do with the unexpected break.

Carol and Melody were delighted by this news, but Iain had a worried look. Carol asked him,

"Why the long face? Don't you want a break?"

"Why should he?" said Melody. "We've been acting all our lives. It's a job to us. It's all new to Iain and still an adventure. He'd rather be hanging about the set and talking to the camera operators even if he did have time off."

"It's all right, I'll be happy to show you around. Anyway, I'd like to go up to Glen Clairaig. Some of the local WFF folk are usually there, looking out for the birds. I'd like to ask them if they know anything about what happened."

"If they're not in jail by then," said Carol.

Iain glared at her. Some of them were his friends, people he'd known all his life.

"Look," he said, scowling, "none of these people would ever do anything to hurt an animal – or a human being either!"

"Sorry… I didn't mean anything by it. It was just a silly joke."

Iain's face brightened and he even smiled.

"The thing is, I'd better go home tonight after all. You see my big sister's in the WFF. My parents might get worried about her if they hear some muddled version before I can tell them what's really happened. I'll come back here first thing tomorrow morning and we can all cycle up to the glen together. It's lovely up there and you'll see the old broch too. It's well worth a visit." He grinned at the others. "You know it's haunted too… by a headless ghost with a great bloody axe!"

FOUR

EAGLES OVER THE GLEN

When Iain met the others in the morning, he was carrying a shoulder bag packed with sandwiches and juice. The twins also carried refreshments and Carol had copies of their scripts. They were not to escape their work altogether. They set off on their bikes and made their way along the country road that led up to the glen. After a while, the road narrowed and they found themselves following a long and winding track, uphill all the way. The sun was now higher in the sky and the morning coolness had gone, so that they began to swelter in the summer heat. They got off their bikes and pushed them uphill, leaning on them for support.

"*Phew!* This hill goes on for ever," groaned Melody. "Can't we stop for a rest?"

"There's a little place, just around the next corner I think," said Iain, "where they've cut a space and laid out benches. It's so the tourists can look out and admire the view."

"Well, we're tourists, sort of, and I'll be happy to admire the view if I can just sit down for a bit."

The view was quite wonderful. From the bench where they sat, munching sandwiches, they could look right down the glen. In the distance was a loch, a glimmering sheet of water, shaded by mountains on one side and a dense wood on the other. Further away they could see low hills marking the end of the glen and in a gap between the hills they caught a glimpse of the distant sea.

"Look," said Iain, pointing to a greyish object that stood on top of a mound overlooking the loch, "there's the broch."

Carol delved into her bag and produced a small pair of binoculars.

"Yes… you were right, Melody, it does look like the tower of a castle – only round and much fatter."

"It's been restored a bit," said Iain. "Half of it used to be just stones lying about the hillside. Now it's almost complete… at least on the outside. There's still work to be done inside."

"It would be wonderful if inside it was just like when it was first built, with all the rooms and… well whatever they had inside them."

"They might fix that one day if they get more money. That was the plan at first, but they ran out." Iain turned and grinned at the others. "And of course, the workmen didn't want to stay any longer because of the ghost!"

"Ha! Ha!" said Melody, sarcastically. "You're just pulling our legs."

"Well, I think we should *stretch* our legs now," said Carol, "and get going. I'd like to see that brock – *brocksh* – whatever you call it – close up."

They had another short climb, which they managed without too much difficulty, as the road wasn't so steep as before. Then they were flying downhill, wind blowing in their hair, and constantly having to use their brakes to keep their bikes under control on the narrow, twisting downhill track.

A half hour later they had reached the mound by the loch and stood looking up at the broch. It was an eerie, unfriendly sort of building with no windows to speak of. It looked gloomy and forbidding even in the afternoon sunshine.

"Brrrr!" said Melody. "I don't like that place. Is it really haunted?"

"Not really," Iain told her. "It's just stories they put in the booklets for tourists to make the place seem more interesting."

"Seems to me," said Carol, "that it's interesting enough as it is. You can just imagine the ancient warriors standing guard up there long ago. That door looks a bit too modern though."

Iain laughed.

"When they finished repairing the outside, they stuck that door in to stop anyone from getting in."

Melody lay down, leaning against the slope.

"The sun's lovely. Let's just rest for a bit – we've got plenty of time."

Carol got out the scripts and threw one at her.

"Lazy sod! This is just the right time to have a read through."

The sun was too gloriously hot, however. They couldn't concentrate to do more than skim their lines before they dozed off, scripts over their faces as sunshades.

Iain sat up suddenly. He looked back along the track but could see nothing. Then he glanced at his watch. He gave his two friends a shove.

"Wake up! It's time we were going."

They got their bikes and pedalled onwards, the road rising once more but not too steeply. As they 'whirred along' – as Melody called it, referring to the sound their wheels made as they sped along the road – they talked, calling over shoulders or coming up, side-by-side, to speak. The road was very quiet with no sign of a bike or a car or even a lonely hiker for miles ahead or miles behind.

After a while, they heard the sound of a motor behind them. They glanced back.

"I can't see anything," said Melody. "But I hear something. It's getting louder."

"It's probably miles away," Iain called back to her. "This glen's so quiet and so wide open, every little sound carries for miles and miles."

They cycled on for a bit. When they glanced back again, they saw a thin cloud of dust puffing up in the distance. The noise of the motor was louder now. Something was coming and it was on the same narrow road that they were on.

"Keep single file, everyone," Iain shouted.

He pushed ahead, moving close to the narrow road's verge. The others moved in behind him. A few seconds later they could hear the roar of the car engine close behind them. Carol, at the rear, shouted forward.

"It must be going at a tremendous rate to have caught up with us so soon."

She glanced back at the onrushing vehicle. It was a grey SUV – she had no time however to notice anything else, except for one thing. They were on a single lane road with barely enough width for such a large vehicle.

"Look out!" she shouted again. "He's not giving us any room!"

The machine rushed by them, so close that the wind of its passing unsettled them on their bikes, making them wobble frantically. And worse. They had just come to a bend in the road, and the car turned sharply. Its wing mirror caught the edge of Iain's handlebars. His front wheel spun round sharply and he had to leap off his bike before he fell under it. Even so he couldn't keep his feet and fell into a bunch of heather. The other two stopped and helped him up.

"Are you hurt?" asked Melody. "Oh, you're scratched."

"It's nothing really. Did you get his number?"

They both shook their heads.

"Sorry," said Carol. "It was going too fast. Then I was worried about you. It's lucky you fell into that clump of heather. Look at all the stones lying about here – if you'd fell on one you could have been badly injured."

"Well, I'm OK. I'd better check my bike."

While he was bent over, examining the wheels, Melody pulled little bits of heather from his hair.

"I caught a glimpse of a man in the passenger seat. He was quite bald – at least his head was. He had a beard."

"No hair on top – plenty of hair below," said Carol. "An upside-down character!"

"Do you know whose car that was, Iain?"

"I didn't recognise it. Anyway, nobody from

around here would drive like that with cyclists on the road. They must be strangers."

"They were in an awful hurry. Where do you think they were going?"

"The only place that way is *An Sloc Beag* – that's a little hollow, at the end of the glen. There are some big houses there, mostly owned by rich folk who've retired here."

"Maybe they're staying there," suggested Melody, "or work for someone there."

"If they do, they're well out of their way. The main road through Ardriagh would get them there quicker. This road goes round the back way and is a lot longer."

"Maybe not, the way they were driving," said Carol. "They couldn't drive like that on a proper road with other cars about."

"Forget about them!" said Melody. "If you're all right, Iain, let's get on."

They set off and soon forgot the car and the near accident. After a while they turned off the road and pedalled their way up a narrower, twisting path that seemed to be designed more for sheep than anything else. Halfway up they had to dismount and push their bikes for a little while. It was much harder and steeper than the first time they had done this earlier in the morning. But they didn't have to push for too long this time. Hardly another ten minutes had passed when they turned a narrow, twisty corner and came across a group of young people camped on a level area to the side of the path. Two came over. One was a fair-haired lad in his late teens, the other a dark-haired girl, who looked much younger. The girl grabbed Iain and ruffled his hair.

"How's my little film-star brother?"

Iain pushed her away and the older boy laughed.

"Have you come up to see our eagles?" he asked.

"Yes, we were hoping we might get a look at them." Iain introduced the twins. "Carol, Melody – I suppose you recognise them. This is Davy and my sister Kirsty. Her boyfriend Calum's somewhere about. She's nearly sixteen by the way, even if she doesn't look much older than you two."

Kirsty scowled at her brother then swiftly put on a smile for the other girls.

"Did you hear about the trouble down at the Laird's place?" asked Melody.

"Oh yes," Kirsty's scowl reappeared, "we heard all about it. We're all criminals and they'll be sending the police to arrest us soon."

"Don't be daft!" replied Iain. "You know the Laird has a terrible temper but when his sister, Lady Agnes, gets back…"

"Lady Agnes can go jump in the loch!"

Iain lost his temper and shouted back at her. Davy grabbed Iain with one hand and Kirsty with the other. He gave them both a good shaking – he was tall and strong and the pair were small and light.

"Look, you two, behave! Now calm down, Iain, and tell us all you know about what happened. You keep quiet too, Kirsty, till he's finished."

Carol and Melody grinned at this. They could barely stop themselves from laughing at Iain being shaken about. Iain did calm down however and told Davy what had happened. He finished by saying,

"The police will want to speak to you and the others. But they don't have any evidence apart from the badge they found. Anyone could get one of them, though – it doesn't prove anything."

"Thanks, Iain, it's good to know exactly what happened and not have to rely on rumours. Anyway, we don't really care what trouble the Laird stirs up. It will be good publicity for us in the WFF when it's proved we didn't do anything…"

"Because we didn't!" said Kirsty, clenching her fist.

"I don't think anybody thinks that, apart from the Laird," said Iain, "not even the police. I'm sure the Laird will realise that once he calms down. He's always losing his temper about something."

Kirsty laughed at this and it seemed they had made up.

"Well then," said Davy, "some of us will go down to Ardriagh to see the police. We'll remind them how we helped catch these poachers a while back – the ones that were using dynamite. We helped them and the Laird then. But that can wait. Come round with us to the hide and we'll see if the eagles are up to anything. That lassie – Melody, isn't it – had better borrow my jacket, that shirt of hers is bright enough to be seen from the other end of the glen."

Melody blushed as she took the proffered jacket, but Kirsty laughed and said,

"Don't be daft, the poor wee thing will be buried under that big coat of yours. Here, take mine instead."

The others tried to hide smiles at Kirsty calling Melody 'wee', for although she was older, she was hardly much taller than her or Carol. Anyway, Kirsty's jacket fitted her snugly. So off they went round the next bend and ahead of them they saw the hide. It looked like a small hut made of stones and wood, but they could see that the front of it was covered with turfs and leafy branches so that it would be difficult for any animal coming from that direction to spot it. Inside the hide, it was gloomy but cool and rather refreshing after their climb in the hot sun. Another girl was peering out through enormous binoculars fixed to a narrow slit facing a high cliff opposite them. She turned and grinned.

"You're just in time, they're feeding the eaglets just now."

"You must be Davy's sister!" said Melody. "You're very like him."

"Aye, I'm Morag. Here: have a look-see."

She waved them over and let them look through the binoculars one at a time.

"Oh! I can see a baby eagle!" Melody was ecstatic.

"These are really powerful," said Iain. "The eagles look like specks in the sky but with the binoculars you can see them as clear as anything."

"Surely," Melody asked, "nobody could get near the eagles, away up there on top of the cliff?"

"It looks impossible from this side but it's not so hard from the north side. It's still difficult but a good climber could do it. Don't worry though, we have people keeping an eye on things over there too. We keep in touch using these."

He pulled a hand-sized, black and yellow object from a bag.

"A two-way radio!" Carol exclaimed. "It looks really cool."

"That's just like the ones the mountain rescue team use," said Iain. "They really need them because you can't always get a mobile signal up here."

"Yes. They told us how good they are – they've a range of ten kilometres. "Look, you can have this one. We bought more than we needed; it's a spare."

"Thanks a lot!"

Iain took it eagerly and Davy explained all the settings.

"We're divided into groups and each group has their own frequency. We don't use this one: it's the same frequency that your film crew use. Look, I've set this to your sister's group so you can talk to her – or Calum – if you want."

At that moment, Calum entered, grinning. He was a short but well-built teenager with reddish brown hair. Iain rolled his eyes as Calum gave Kirsty a peck on the cheek.

"They'll be in a group of two, I suppose. Can they keep their eyes off each other long enough to watch the eagles?"

Kirsty gave him a thump but moments later she joined in the general laughter.

They spent nearly two hours in the hide, looking at the eagles mostly, but occasionally seeing other animals – a fox, hares, a pine marten and once, just briefly, some deer. They had a snack and late in the afternoon set off back to the manor, looking forward to getting back and having a good dinner.

FIVE

PESTERED BY THE PRESS

The next morning was hectic. Oswald had arranged for extra scenes to be filmed to make up for lost time. Lunch was brief, and only lasted half an hour before they were back filming. They all felt rushed and flustered but in a funny way everyone seemed to be at the top of their form. The children's scenes were finished by 2 pm. They were so exhausted they just flopped down on couches and armchairs in the big lounge the actors used as a 'break room'.

"That was great fun," said Carol, "but I'm wasted."

"Me too," said Iain. "I'm glad I can stay overnight – I'm too shattered to cycle back to the village. Anyway, my parents are away at Inverness visiting my Aunt Sheona, so I'd be stuck with my sister."

"I suppose Kirsty is out in the glen again," said Melody.

Before Iain could answer, Jamie the caretaker stuck his head through the door. He grinned at the sight of them, all draped about armchairs.

"Iain, you'll have to stir yourself. Your sister's on the phone."

Iain sat up, all at once alert.

"Kirsty?" He leapt to his feet. "What's happened?"

"No idea. She didn't say."

Iain rushed out of the room, suddenly full of energy. The twins exchanged glances but they were too tired to even think of a comment. Five minutes later Iain reappeared.

"I'll have to go into town," he told them. "Kirsty's gone to Ardriagh with Calum and Davy to speak to the police. But she's such a goose, she's gone and left her keys at home and of course Mum and Dad are away. I'd better go now, in case she goes back and breaks in through one of our windows. See you later."

Carol and Melody got up, slowly but with determined expressions.

"I've been meaning to go into town," said Carol.

"There are a few things I want to get."

"I'm coming too. We should all go and give her our support."

"If she's not in a cell," said Carol, putting her fingers across her face as if she was looking out through bars. Iain couldn't help but laugh, though he didn't really want to see his sister in prison.

"She's too young to go to prison," Melody said. "So are most of them. Anyway, there's no real evidence against them."

"Innocent people have been sent to prison before," said Carol.

"Oh, *shut up*, Carol!" Melody glanced at the clock. "Look at the time – we may have missed the bus already."

"We can make it if we cycle down to the bus stop," said Iain. Without waiting for a reply, he rushed off to his room to get his keys. His friends stood looking after him for a moment, then they too rushed off.

They just made it. The bus was coming down the road as they arrived at the stop. They left their bikes, clambered on and settled down to get their breath back. They all wore T-shirts and shorts, but Carol and Melody had put on sunglasses and skip caps. The latter were pulled down to partially hide their faces. Iain asked them why they were doing this, as they didn't usually bother about being noticed.

"We're here to give Kirsty our support," said Melody. "We don't want to be distracted by anything else, like autograph hunters or reporters."

Half an hour later they saw the outskirts of Ardriagh approaching and they were soon walking up Main Street in the town.

"I think you should phone your sister," said Melody. "Our mobiles will work now we're in town."

"Good idea!" Iain looked around. "Let's find a quiet spot so I don't have to shout down the phone. Over there will do."

They went down a short, narrow lane away from busy Main Street. At a low wall that overlooked a pebbly shore and a slowly incoming tide, Iain reached for his mobile. A voice rang out.

"Iain! Iain Fraser!"

He looked up to see two children running towards him, both very brown and both obviously brother and sister. The boy was slightly taller and much plumper. They wore jeans and T-shirts: the boy's top was dark blue with a large picture of the moon printed on it; the girl's was sky blue with the image of a bright yellow sun.

"Raj! Raveena! What are you doing here? I thought you were on holiday in Spain."

"Our mum was ill," said Raj, "so we had to come home early."

"Oh no! That's terrible… how is she?" Iain realised that they were grinning too widely for

47

children whose mum was seriously ill. "She *is* fine, isn't she?"

"Yes. We were really worried at first…"

"Mum was in awful pain," Raveena's grin faded as she remembered how badly she'd felt then, "but once she got to hospital, they found it wasn't as serious as we thought. They fixed her up fine."

"Dad's taken her on another holiday – a quiet holiday, so she can get lots of rest. He sent us back to stay with our Aunt Nyra – he said Mum wouldn't get any peace with us around."

Raveena gave a coy glance at Iain's companions.

"Why don't you introduce us to your new friends?"

Iain realised she had seen through their minimal disguise.

"Carol, Melody – this is Rajneesh and Raveena Akash. They're in my class at the village school. Raveena's a year younger than us but the school's so small that kids of different ages are taught in the same class."

Melody took off her sunglasses and smiled, giving a little wave of her hand. Carol grinned. Raveena was thrilled and jumped up and down like a much younger little girl.

"It really is you! Your pictures are on display at the community centre, with all the other actors in the film you're making."

"Yours too, Iain," said Raj. "You're a big star now."

Iain felt his face burning. He was lost for words

but was saved further embarrassment when his phone beeped. He answered the call.

"Kirsty? What's up?"

Kirsty's voice could be heard but the others couldn't make out what she said.

"What are you talking about? What crowd?" Iain looked more and more anxious as he listened. "OK, I'll meet you there."

"What on earth has happened?" asked Melody.

"There's a huge bunch of reporters at the station. They heard about our friends being questioned by the police and they're mobbing the place."

"We can't have that many reporters in Ardriagh," said Raj. "Where did they all come from?"

"A lot of reporters from the big towns are here because we're making the film," said Melody. "I suppose mixing film stars and escaped wild animals makes a great story."

"Escaped wild animals?" Raj was surprised and curious. "From the Laird's zoo, you mean?"

"Look, I really have to meet Kirsty. I'll tell you all about it if you walk with us."

They strode along the embankment at a brisk pace while Iain – with interruptions from Carol and Melody – told the whole story about the escaped animals and their own close call with the wild ape.

"Wow! That was a narrow escape," said Raveena. "You weren't hurt, were you, Iain?"

She clasped his hand and put her other hand on

his shoulder, as if comforting a close friend.

"Not really. I'm fine now."

Now Iain explained how the Laird had blamed his friends in the WFF and because of this they'd had to come and speak to the police.

"But Kirsty forgot her house keys and I've had to come in to let her borrow mine."

"Just like sisters," said Raj. Then, "Ouch!" as his punched him.

Approaching the station, they saw that Kirsty had not exaggerated about the number of reporters waiting outside.

"Jumping giraffes!" said Carol. "Look at the crowd of them. Let's hope they don't spot us."

"Carol – Melody – you'd better stay out of sight and I'll go in myself," said Iain. "They're bound to recognise you."

"You might get recognised yourself, Iain," said Raj. "Your picture was up with all the other actors."

"I've an idea," said Raveena. "Why don't Raj and I go in with Iain? If he keeps his head down they'll only notice us and we're not famous."

"It might work," said Melody, "but what about when you come out? They'll still want to pester your sister and her friends."

"I know!" Carol beamed a broad smile. "You three go ahead. When you're leaving phone me, and Mel and I will distract the reporters."

Melody looked askance. Carol always had

hairbrained ideas. She hoped this wasn't one of her really silly ones. However she didn't want to let her friends down so she just nodded. Iain borrowed Carol's skip cap and pulled the peak down. Accompanied by the Akashs, he walked over to the main entrance, his head down. As they neared the reporters Raj began to talk loudly about his holiday in Spain – the good part, before his mother became ill. Raveena joined in and Iain nodded from time to time. They seemed so much like ordinary children that the reporters paid them no attention. Then, just as they were almost at the door, one reporter blocked their way. He was a thin, narrow-eyed man with stubble on his face, and untidily dressed.

"What are you kids going in there for? You got anything to do with the WFF?"

Iain kept his head down but Raj looked up, showing the bright white moon on his T-shirt.

"No. We're going in to report a lost cow. It jumped over me and ran away with the spoons."

It wasn't much of a joke but the sleazy-looking reporter must have been unpopular with the others for they all laughed uproariously.

"Better write that up right away, Weasel," said one. "It's big news!"

This distraction let the children slip through the door and they were soon directed to a room where their friends were waiting.

"It's about time you got here!" Kirsty declared.

"Oh, thank you very much dear brother for helping me out," Iain said in a sarcastic voice. "It was a real bother getting in past all these reporters. I might not have made it without Raj and his sister's help. Here's my keys – don't lose *them*."

Before Kirsty could throw an insult back at him, a policeman stuck his head through the door.

"Right, miss, you and your friends will have to leave now. Your brother has brought your keys and that mob outside are blocking our entrance."

"Oh no! What will we do?"

Calum spoke up.

"Maybe we could barge through them like a rugby maul."

"Don't be daft," said Davy. "We don't want to be pestered by them just now but we don't want to antagonise them either. They'll make out we are real troublemakers if we did that."

"I can get rid of them," said Iain, taking out his mobile.

"You!?" Calum and Kirsty laughed.

Iain dialled Carol and simply said: "Now's the time."

Then, ignoring the rest, he walked out. He stopped at the exit and peered out to look at the crowd of reporters. He held up a hand to tell the others to wait, then he grinned. The crowd was beginning to disperse as the reporters moved off. When the others looked out the entrance was almost clear.

"How on earth did you do that?" asked Davy, quite astonished – as were the other WFF members, including Calum and Kirsty.

Carol put away her mobile and grabbed Melody by the arm.

"We're on!" she said.

They walked over to the station and as they got near, Carol waved her arm and shouted.

"Hey! We've come to see our friends in the WFF and help them out."

For a moment the reporters were too surprised to react. Then one shouted out,

"It's the kids from the movie – they're based at the place where the animals escaped."

Before he had finished speaking, the crowd broke up and reformed into a rushing pack. Carol and Melody turned and hurried away – but not far. Carol had spotted a plinth, supporting a statue that vaguely resembled the wings of a large bird. They climbed up and each sat on a wing, looking down on the crowd surrounding them. The reporters gathered round them, some taking pictures. Carol had judged the position perfectly. It was the kind of set up media people loved for photographs and it meant the reporters would turn their backs to the station entrance. Even as she began to speak to her audience, Carol could see her friends leaving quietly, quite unnoticed by anyone. She could only manage a quick glance because the reporters began to throw all sorts of questions at her and her sister.

"How many animals escaped?" "Was anyone attacked?" "Is the public in any danger?" "Will the film company be sued?"

Some of the questions were needless, even silly, but they answered as best they could, or at least Carol did most of the time. Then they were asked,

"Did you see any of the escaped animals yourselves?"

Carol grinned from ear to ear. "Yes, we did – in fact we had a narrow escape."

She enjoyed telling them about their adventure with the wild ape, though this time she made them all out to have been braver than they actually had been. Melody began to wonder now how on earth they would get away. And she was beginning to wonder what Oswald would think of them giving an unofficial interview to the press. Just then she became aware of a figure climbing up behind her.

"Who's that?" shouted a reporter.

"Davy!"

Melody couldn't help crying out in surprise. Then, questioned, she told them he was from the WFF. This led to a flurry of more photographs and more questions. The two young film stars knowing – even being friends with – the WFF was a new slant and one that would spice up their reports. Davy answered also, making sure they knew they had visited the police voluntarily and there were no charges against them.

"The WFF is all about protecting animals, we would never do anything to harm them. I can let you have some leaflets about what we do up here."

The reporters were not much interested in this. They already had plenty of material for really good stories, so they quickly broke up and dispersed to get their copy in. Melody was relieved but Carol was a little disappointed and felt things would be dull for a while after that excitement. She was wrong.

"Come with me," Davy told them. "The others are waiting at Carlos's Continental Café."

As they strolled along, Carol asked Davy why he had avoided the press before when he had no problem speaking to them just then.

"We'd have been squeezed into a tiny space at that entrance and we'd have all felt under pressure. There are one or two WFF members who are liable to say or do something silly…"

"Like Kirsty?" said Carol with a grin.

"I see you take Iain's side but yes, she's one. Calum's a bit hot-headed too. I didn't want anyone to say anything to turn the press against us – or say anything against the Laird. That would just turn him even more against us. We need to prove he's wrong about us first."

They were coming up to the café, where they could see their friends sitting outside.

"That was a smart move of yours, by the way. It

got us out without any bother and let me give our side of the story to the press."

"No problem." Carol beamed. "I've got a lot of experience dealing with the press, so I knew how to handle the situation."

"Yes," said Melody. "You were rather brilliant doing that all by yourself."

Carol had the grace to look a little embarrassed for of course Melody had helped and Iain and the Akashs had played their part too. At the café, Davy and most of his WFF friends quickly swallowed their last dregs of coffee and made their goodbyes. Davy was old enough to drive and was allowed to use his father's Landrover; he was their lift home. Kirsty and Calum wanted to spend some time together, so went off by themselves hand-in-hand.

"Well," said Iain, getting up, "I suppose, we'd better get back now."

"Wait a bit!" said Carol. "I want to get some magazines or a book. I've read everything worth reading at the manor."

Iain checked his watch.

"Oh! We've just missed a bus. It'll be an hour till the next one."

"Never mind," said Carol. "We can get something to eat in town."

"Good plan!" said Iain. "We've had enough excitement today."

But they hadn't.

SIX

TROUBLE IN TOWN

They wandered along the promenade for a bit. Earlier they had been in a rush but now they could take their time, enjoying the view and the sun on their faces. Soon they were all feeling empty inside and decided to move on to Main Street where most of the shops were to be found.

"Raj, you know the town," said Carol. "Where's the nearest newsagent?"

"My uncle runs one on Main Street. There's a chip shop close by too."

"Do your parents own a shop, too?"

"No, our dad's a doctor. He has a practice here in town but we live in Laganglas, like Iain. My mum works part-time in a nursery here."

Iain and Raj led the way, taking a circuitous route through narrow alleys.

"Iain and Raj seem to be good friends," Melody said to Raveena. "They're chatting away like anything."

"Everyone's quite pally where we come from – it's such a small place. But Iain and Raj have become really close ever since they were put in charge of the school magazine last year. They more or less run it together."

"I knew Iain likes to write stories – so Raj writes too?"

"Oh no!" Raveena laughed. "He's mad on computers. He's the only one who knows how to run their desktop publishing program and get the magazine printed properly."

"That's awesome! But what will the school do next year? Raj and Iain will be at secondary school by then."

Raveena laughed even louder than before.

"He tells everyone he's training up Miss Stewart to take over. He'll still be able to help, though, because the files are all saved to a cloud so he can edit stuff from anywhere."

"Look out! We're falling behind. Run!"

They caught up with the boys just as they were going into a particularly narrow and twisty lane. It was so narrow that it seemed quite dark after the bright sunshine of the more open spaces. Halfway through they heard a sudden yell followed by a loud voice.

"Shut him up!"

Without thinking, the children ran forward round the curve of the lane. There they had a shock. Two men stood over a third who was lying on the ground. He was holding a hand to his head and blood trickled through his fingers from a nasty cut. The standing men turned, surprised to see that they had five young witnesses to their assault on the other man. One of the men was bald and wore sunglasses; he also had a thick, dark beard. He looked for a moment as if he would attack them too. Then Melody had an inspiration. She ran back a few paces and shouted, as if she was calling to someone just round the bend of the lane.

"Mum! Dad! Someone's being attacked here. Call the police!"

The bearded thug hesitated for a moment, but he didn't attack them. Melody's trick had worked.

"Leave it!" he told his companion. Then, he leaned over the man on the ground.

"Don't you forget what we said."

The two men ran off. Iain started to run after them but Carol caught him and pulled him back.

"Iain, you donkey! Don't you ever think before you rush into things? What if you caught up with these men? They would have battered you."

Rather abashed, Iain joined his friends gathered round the injured man. Melody stood a little apart, her mobile at her ear – she was calling for an ambulance.

"That was really smart of you, Mel," Raj said.

She ignored him and asked Raveena what the lane they were in was called, then passed this on to the emergency services person.

"That's right," she said, "he's bleeding and doesn't seem to be able to get up."

Iain tried to clean the blood from the injured man's head, without much success. Every time he dabbed at the wound, the man winced with pain. Carol, leaning over, got a glimpse of his face for the first time and cried out in astonishment.

"That's Harry! That's Harry Puddock!"

Melody leaned over for a closer look. She gave a little shriek.

"You're right, it is him. Oh Harry! What have they done to you?"

Carol answered the puzzled expressions of the Akashs, telling them about Harry.

"He makes artefacts – jewellery, daggers, goblets, things like that – to be used in the movie."

Harry seemed to come to his senses a little, but at the same time became agitated. His eyes flashed round the children's faces, then he stared at Melody – the first face he recognised. He feebly tried to push Iain away and croaked out her name.

"Mel… Melody. Keep some… thing… for me."

Groaning with an effort which obviously caused

him some pain, and with a bit of a struggle, he drew out a small case from his jacket pocket.

"Take this… please. Keep it for me… for a bit. Don't let anyone…"

Melody grabbed the case as it was slipping out of his hand. Harry seemed in a bad way. He slumped back against the wall and though his eyes were still open, he didn't seem to be looking at anything.

"Hold him," said Raj, "he's going to fall down."

With Iain's help, he kept him sitting upright while Raveena rubbed his hands, which seemed to be getting very cold. Then they heard the sound of an ambulance siren and moments later an ambulance appeared at the head of the lane. It stopped there and the paramedics came along with a stretcher. They worked quickly and efficiently. Harry's wound was cleaned and bandaged then he was carried into the back of the ambulance. When the doors were closed, the driver-paramedic told them,

"Someone obviously assaulted this man. We'll have to inform the police. They'll want to speak to you."

"As if we hadn't seen enough of the police," groaned Iain. "Now I suppose we'll have to go to the station again."

As luck would have it a policeman and policewoman, patrolling nearby, appeared just in time to have a quick word with the driver. Then they spoke to the children, and took their names and addresses (amused to discover two of their witnesses were familiar from television).

"Did you see what the attackers looked like?" the policewoman asked. "No, don't all speak at once – you, Melody, what did you see?"

The police constable shook her head when she described the bearded man.

"It's something, but I'm afraid a beard and sunglasses pretty much hides a face. Lots of young men shave their heads nowadays too."

"You know, Iain," said Melody, "the man I saw in the car that nearly ran you down the other day had a beard and was bald too."

"You think it was the same man?" The policewoman looked askance at her again.

"I don't know for sure. I couldn't get a good look because the car was going so fast."

"We heard one of them shout," said Carol. "He sounded like he had a London accent. I'm quite good at accents."

The policewoman scribbled in her notebook, muttering to herself.

"Hmm! There are a lot of tourists around just now, some from London. We'll keep a lookout for them but they'll probably leave the area if they know they've been seen."

They were quite relieved when the police constables let them go. They had been hungry before but after the latest excitement and delay they were famished.

"Let's find that chip shop," said Carol. "I'll get my magazines later."

They bought their food and wandered back to the promenade overlooking the shore. There, they sat on the low wall, stuffing themselves with chips or fritters, and bites of pie, hamburger or haddock, depending on what had taken their fancy. Raveena suddenly jumped down. She stuffed the remains of her meal in a nearby bin. With a little hop and skip she came back, her mobile in her hand.

"We need to get a selfie of us all together," she squealed.

"There's five of us," said Iain. "Wouldn't we need one of these selfie-stick things?"

"Not if we all squash together," said Raveena, giggling. "Who's got the longest arm?"

Carol grabbed the mobile before anyone could argue – though she was the same size as her sister – and everyone squeezed together around her. The first attempt was a disaster, with more of the tops of their heads showing than anything. Raveena started giggling and her giggle was so infectious that they were all soon giggling and laughing. Somehow at last they managed to get some decent photos.

"These are good," said Raj. "I'll put them up on my Prince of the Night page."

"Your what?" Carol asked.

"It's his personal web page," said Iain. "He prefers

it to Facebook."

"Let's me do more and I can link to any other media I like."

"Why do you call it 'Prince of the Night'?" asked Melody.

"It's what his name means," said Raveena. "Mine means 'Beautiful Sun'."

She tilted her head to one side, as if she was posing for a photograph.

"You would make a fine model," said Melody. "You're definitely pretty enough."

Raveena began to dance, her arms above her head with her fingers wriggling.

"I'd really like to be in a Bollywood movie, singing and dancing."

"Well, please don't sing now," said Raj. "I haven't got anything to plug my ears with."

Raveena gave her brother a good-natured thump. Then she grabbed Iain by the arm and said,

"You really ought to write something about what it's like to be a film star – it would be a great article for the school magazine."

"I'm not a film star! I'm just… well no one's seen the film yet so no one knows anything about me."

"But it must be marvellous being filmed, dressing up and acting – and getting to know all these famous actors."

"Yes," said Carol, grinning. "He really thinks it's wonderful knowing stars like me."

"Big-head!" said Iain and Melody together.

"I was just kidding. I think Raveena's trying to drop us a hint. She'd love to come up to the manor and meet some of the cast."

"I can't think why she shouldn't," said Melody. "We've had friends visit us when we've been filming other movies."

"I'm sure it wouldn't be a problem, as long as we're filming at the manor or the Barn studio and not on location."

"What about you, Raj?" asked Iain. "Do you want to come too?"

"Are you kidding? Of course I'll come. Do you think they'd let me take some photos of you all filming?"

"It might be OK to take photos of behind the scenes. You know, the cameramen, sound people; all that kind of stuff."

Carol and Melody were surprised to find that Raj was quite pleased with that idea. They promised to arrange things as soon as they could.

"We'll get in touch with you as soon as everything's settled," said Carol.

"Iain knows my number," said Raj. "So he can phone me when you've fixed things up."

"Don't be a donkey, Raj," said his sister. "We're staying with Aunt Nyra – so he'll have to phone us at her home using a landline telephone."

Raj flashed a scowl which was replaced almost at once by an embarrassed grin.

"Here," he said to Iain, "I'll text you my aunt's number. If we're not in, leave a message."

They wandered about the town for a bit, chatting and exchanging stories until it was time for the young actors to get their bus. Their farewells were quite cheerful for they had shared some exciting moments and knew they would be meeting up again soon.

All the way back to the manor they talked about the afternoon's events. Carol went on for a bit about what she called her 'press conference'. But the other two soon got fed up listening to her tell them how clever she had been. Melody tried to change the subject.

"Your friends, Raj and Raveena, are quite a pair, Iain. I had a really good time with them, especially Raveena. It was nice to have another girl for company for once."

"What am I then?" asked Carol. "Your poodle?"

"You might as well be a boy. Anyway you don't count, you're my skin and blister!"

"Oh, very cockney!" Carol laughed, not in the least bothered.

"Raj was quite smart when that reporter tried to block our way into the station," said Iain. "The other reporters didn't think much of him, though. They called him the Weasel."

"The Weasel!" Melody laughed. "Why did they call him that."

"I don't know – perhaps because he looked a bit weaselly?" Iain described the reporter to her.

"He sounds a bit sleazy – the kind of reporter who'll do any dirty trick to get a story!"

"I don't understand. What do you mean?"

Melody laughed, a cold humourless laugh.

"Reporters can be a pest," said Carol, "though most are not too bad. But there are a few who will go to any length to get a story."

"Our mum's an actress too," said Melody, "and she had a horrible reporter follow her about for weeks. He pestered neighbours and friends to try to get some gossip about her."

"Oh! I see," said Iain. "I suppose we'd better keep a look out for him."

"Oh, Oswald's very careful about reporters nowadays. You see, when he was making a film a couple of years ago, some rat of a reporter sneaked into the dressing rooms and stole actors' personal stuff including letters. Just so he could write some nasty stuff for his newspaper. Ugh! My skin's crawling just thinking about it."

"No reporter will get near his actors now without a pass," said Carol, "and if they try anything dodgy, they're banned."

They sat in silence for a while as this tale about what some reporters got up to had somewhat dampened their mood. Then, as they were nearing the manor, Melody gave a little gasp and put her hand to her mouth. It was a habit she had when she suddenly thought of something. From her pocket, she took out the little case Harry had given her.

"I forgot all about this. I wonder what it is."

"Bus stop's coming up," said Iain. "Move! It's a mile to the next one. We don't want that extra walk."

They tumbled out of the bus and across the road to the opposite stop where their bikes were lying. But while the others fumbled with their bikes, Melody opened the little case. She put her hand to her mouth and squealed.

"What on earth was that for?" asked Carol.

But she didn't need to wait for an answer. Dangling from Melody's fingers was the most dazzling, beautiful, jewelled necklace they had ever seen.

SEVEN

DANGER AT THE BROCH

Carol's mouth gaped wide for long seconds. "Jumping giraffes! Where did Harry get that?"

"That's the kind of thing he makes for the film, isn't it?" said Iain.

"Why would he be carrying it around? All our made-up jewellery is supposed to be kept in the workshop."

"It looks real," said Melody. "Don't give me that look. I know the costumers use artificial jewels which look quite real – but I've seen real jewels."

"Hey! I forgot," said Carol, slapping the top of her own head (then wincing because she'd slapped harder than she meant to). "Ronnie said she left a necklace with Harry to be repaired. That might be it."

"Let's get back first," said Iain, mounting his bike. "If Ronnie's around we can ask her."

"Or check with Harry later," said Melody. "We ought to go and see him in hospital."

"And question him?" Carol asked.

"I don't think we should do that, unless he's a lot better. He was in a bad way – I can imagine they might keep him in for a few days."

"Yes, of course," said Iain. "It depends when we can get free time too."

Although they weren't very hungry, they thought some tea and biscuits would be refreshing, so they went to the dining room.

While they were there, Oswald Wales came in and made a beeline for them.

"Ah! I thought when you eventually turned up I would find you here."

The children groaned, for he had three thick-looking scripts. Oswald gave out a deep, throaty chuckle.

"These aren't for you, don't worry. However, you *will* be wanted tomorrow morning. I've put your scripts in your bedrooms, so read them before you go to sleep, please. You don't have that many lines to speak, so it shouldn't be a problem."

The children suddenly remembered they hadn't told anyone about Harry. They rushed out the story now. At first, Oswald thought they were making it up but he soon realised they were serious, in fact genuinely shocked by what had happened.

"That is worrying news. It's lucky you were there to call for help before anything worse happened to him. Now remember, you have to get up very early tomorrow."

"By the way," said Melody, "we want to have a word with Ronnie. Is she in her room?"

"Yes, but you lot keep away from her. She's got a bad headache and has taken some paracetamol and gone to bed. She needs a good night's rest."

When he had gone, Melody sighed and said,

"We'll have to catch her later. Maybe we can look out Joe, who works with Harry. He might know who the necklace belongs to."

But there was no chance of seeing either Ronnie or Joe the next day. They were dragged out of bed much earlier than usual and driven up the glen in one of the Landrovers used to transport cast. Other vehicles carried adult actors like Martin Trout, Ravi Ansari and

Wendy Forester and a bunch of extras. Behind them were cars towing two large caravans which were used for makeup and changing costumes. At the tail end a van carried cameras and other technical equipment.

"Oh, look!" cried Carol, through a yawn. "We're headed for the brock – *brocksh*. I thought we'd be filming there soon."

"You'd have known that already, if you'd bothered to read your script," said Melody.

"I did – or at least I tried to, but I was so tired I fell asleep."

"Well, you'd better look at it now."

She flung a script in her sister's face.

Arrived at the broch, the children wandered around for a bit while the cameras and other equipment were set up. The door in the broch was forced open and hidden with a dark cloth. It did not look 'medieval' enough for the movie. The sun was soon higher in the sky and the day was warming up.

"I'll leave my backpack inside the door of the broch," said Iain. "I've packed some food in case I get peckish between takes."

"That's a good idea," said Carol. "There's food in the caravans but it'll be bit of a hike to get to them."

"Well, we have to get to them anyway," said Melody. "We need to get made up and costumed down there."

An hour later they were climbing back up the mound to the broch.

Filming got underway with a lot of action taking place close to the broch. Things went very well, though even at the best of times some scenes couldn't be captured in one take. Lines were repeated for close ups and different angles and occasionally someone tripped over a word or even a tuft of grass and the scene had to be done again. Although things had gone well, the children were relieved when Oswald called a short break at eleven o'clock. They were quite tired after such an early start. Oswald chased them from the filming area as he wanted a different set up for the cameras and sound equipment.

"Go round to the back of the brock for a bit," he told them. "And stay out of the way until you're needed."

"A brock is a badger…" began Carol, but Oswald ignored her.

"How about we take our food to the top of the tower?" said Iain. "We'll be out of the way there and we'll hear you a lot easier when you call for us."

"Fine, fine. Just go."

A stairway of narrow wooden steps had been built so it was possible to climb all the way to the top. Here a small platform had been built, which had a wooden frame on the inner side as a safety barrier.

"What a view!" said Melody. "I'm glad I brought my mobile. There's no signal but I can take some great pictures from here."

"Eat first!" said Carol.

They had all brought different kinds of food, more than any one of them needed, so they shared with each other, while peering over the rampart to watch the crew moving equipment about. They soon got fed up with this and began to scan the glen. In every direction there was a wonderful view. Carol stepped back all of a sudden.

"Some of these stones are loose!" she cried.

Iain examined the wall closely.

"They've rebuilt it the way it was built originally. It's drystane – I mean drystone. All the stones are fitted together so closely they don't need cement, they're sort of locked together and fixed by their whole weight. Some of the small stones are a wee bit loose at the top but…" Melody gave a little squeal when he pulled a stone out which filled the palm of his hand. "See? Nothing moves. This wall is really thick. None of us could lean over it – we'd have to almost lie over it to see directly below us."

Melody looked back and noticed now that a broad netting hung from the wooden frame.

"I suppose," she said, pointing, "that's to stop you dropping stuff over the edge. You don't need it for the outer wall, it's so thick."

She shook crumbs from her fingers, wiped her hands on her costume (which would have infuriated Oswald if he'd seen her), then took out her mobile. She turned slowly, scanning the scenery, taking a snapshot every now and then. Then she stopped and stood still, staring at the image on her camera for a minute.

"There are some odd-looking animals running up from that wood," she said. "They look grey, not white. Are they a special breed of sheep or goats?"

Carol dug out her binoculars from her backpack and peered through them.

"That's not sheep, that's dogs. No! Jumping giraffes! They're wolves!"

They stood in shocked silence for several long moments. Then Melody said,

"They're coming in this direction and moving really fast."

"The zoo fence must have been cut again," said Iain. "We'd better warn them down there."

They all shouted at the top of their voices to warn the crew moving about below. However, they either did not hear them clearly or thought they were playing a game and just ignored them.

"I know," said Iain. He grabbed a couple of loose stones then clambered on top of the wall. He flung a stone down in the direction of the crew which none of them noticed.

"Oh! Be careful," said Melody. "You could kill someone if you hit them from this height."

"You could kill *yourself* if you fall over," said Carol, grabbing his leg to hold him steady.

The second stone hit a camera with a loud *clack*. Luckily it didn't damage it but it did attract the crew's attention. One of the camera operators looked up, shaking a fist at Iain. They all shouted down again about the wolves but they still couldn't make themselves heard.

"Look!" Melody almost screamed the word. "The wolves are getting closer."

"They can't hear us properly," said Carol, "and they can't see the wolves from down there. We can only see them because we're so high up. Come down, Iain, before you fall!"

Iain scrambled down, clumsily falling into Carol and almost knocking her over. A hand Iain put out to keep his balance touched his backpack lying against the wall and he felt something he'd put in it but forgotten. He grabbed the pack and rummaged inside, bringing out the radio Davy had given him.

"What use is that?" asked Melody. But Carol grinned.

"Goose! Don't you remember when Davy showed Iain what all the buttons were for? They don't use one of the frequencies because it's the same one our film crew use. Hurry up, Iain. Call them up before the wolves get here."

Iain switched the radio on and selected the frequency. He had to hold down a button to send a call signal. It only took a few seconds but to the children, who could see the wolf pack getting closer and closer, it seemed like ages. Then a voice crackled from the radio.

"Who's this? What do you want?"

"It's Oswald," Iain told the others.

"Of course it's me – is that you, Iain? Did you nick one of the radios?"

"No! Wait, it's important. We can see something up here that the crew can't. There's a whole lot of wild animals heading towards you – they look like wolves."

"Look, Iain, we've had enough of your nonsense, throwing things—"

"That was to try to attract your attention. We shouted down but they ignored us. If you were up here you'd see them. *Please* listen. We're not kidding."

There was a moment's silence, then he heard Oswald's voice again.

"OK, I'll check it out – but if this *is* a prank you'll all be in for it."

Oswald had been hidden from view among the film equipment. Now they saw him running down the mound.

"Wow!" said Carol. "He can really sprint. Who'd have thought someone his size could move so fast."

"Gravity," said Iain.

"What's he doing?" asked Melody.

It was very soon obvious. He ran back to the little 'camp' of vehicles and jumped into a Landrover. As it drove off at top speed Iain's radio crackled and Oswald's voice came through again. He was talking to all the crew members with radios.

"Listen guys – I'm checking something out that may be a problem. Be ready to get everybody into a safe place. If it turns out to be a false alarm, three pests are going to catch it!"

The Landrover drove out of sight. Minutes later it reappeared, going twice as fast as before. The radio crackled again.

"This is a real EMERGENCY! Everyone take cover now. You are all in danger. Wolves have escaped from the zoo. TAKE COVER!"

"Look!" Melody pointed down to the little 'camp'. "Everyone's getting into a car or a caravan."

Down below, the film crew abandoned their equipment and ran to the broch's entrance.

"I hope that door can still close properly," said Iain. "We've nowhere to go if the wolves get in."

"Don't worry," said Carol, "the wolves will eat the crew down there first. They'll be too full then to bother about us."

"What on earth will we do," asked Melody, "if the wolves don't go away?

"The folk in the cars are OK," said Carol. "They can just drive away – it's the ones downstairs who are stuck."

The wolves had gone out of sight for a bit, hidden by a dip in the ground. They reappeared now, much closer and heading for the mound. They watched in a kind of horrified fascination as they came up and gathered in a pack at the door of the broch, snuffling, barking and growling.

"They must smell the folk inside," said Iain.

He was really worried and thinking frantically, when he suddenly remembered what he had in his hand. He pressed one frequency button after another until he got a reply.

"Who's this?" It was Davy.

"It's me, Iain. Davy, where are you?"

"I'm just starting up the glen. I'm on my bike."

"Great! You can get back to the manor quickly."

Iain quickly explained about the wolves and the film crew's predicament. Davy did not question him, for he'd known Iain for years and knew he wouldn't tell fibs about something so serious. Davy groaned as he listened.

"I bet the Laird will try to blame us for this too. Don't worry – I'm heading back now at top speed. I'll get some of the animal handlers to come out."

They heard noise from down below. Someone shouted.

"Help me with this door. It's stuck and won't close properly!"

The children peered down inside but they could only see vague shapes in the dim depths. It looked like some of the crew were pushing against the door but there was a gap that wouldn't close. Growls and barks, very loud and clear, told them the pack was pushing in at the gap, trying to force their way in.

"This is bad," said Carol. "The wolves could get in before help can arrive."

They stood back and looked desperately around. All their eyes fell at once on the net hanging from the safety frame. They each grabbed a corner of the net where it was loosely tied and stopped. Melody gave a little gasp, as she realised they all had the same idea.

"Everybody get a stone," said Carol. "Then tie each corner to one."

She didn't need explain further because they remembered the TV show where she got this idea from. They took two stones each and in a few minutes had untied the ends of the net from the frame, tied each end to a stone and pulled the net onto the edge of the rampart. They heard a roaring as they did so and looked down.

"Oswald's driving his Landrover up the mound," said Iain. "He's trying to frighten the wolves away."

"That's one way of keeping the wolf from the door," said Carol.

They felt a little disappointed: after all their efforts, there would be no need for their plan. Some of the wolves were distracted by the Landrover, a pair even ran down and barked at it.

"It seems to have slowed down," said Iain. "It's a steep slope but there's something wrong."

There was a splutter and the vehicle's engine died. The Landrover was stuck. More of the wolves moved down, curious and menacing at the same time.

"Come on," said Carol. "We need those wolves back here. Shout, whistle, do anything!"

And they did. They screeched, whistled and bawled. Carol even barked and howled. The wolves were puzzled, but curious, and padded back to towards the wall of the broch. The children continued to make odd noises, especially barks and howls which seemed to attract the wolves more than anything.

"NOW!"

Carol shouted and they flung the stones attached to the net over the wall. Part of the net with stones attached had already been draped over the wall, so as the other end was flung out, it opened out into a great flat web. The wolves stared curiously at it for long seconds. Then as it rushed faster and faster towards them, one of them yelped and turned to get away. The rest of the pack began to move too, but it was too late. Their instinct to stay in a pack betrayed them. The net fell over them, trapping them – except for one wolf which crawled out from under and ran off in a panic. The other wolves struggled aimlessly but only managed to get themselves more tangled in the net. The film crew ran out and, using pegs and clips normally used to fix film equipment in place, they pinned the net securely to the ground.

EIGHT

QUESTIONS AND REVELATIONS

"I owe you kids an apology," said Oswald. "You certainly saved the day. That was really quick thinking."

The animal handlers arrived and moved the wolves into a van to take them back to the zoo. Davy arrived soon after and he too congratulated the children who were feeling very pleased with themselves by now.

"Once we've got these animals back," said Jimmy Cullen, "we'll have to form a hunting party for the wolf that got away. We'll have to issue a warning, too, to warn any folk who visit the glen to be very careful."

Although the cast and crew were relieved by their narrow escape, Oswald was furious. He had lost valuable filming time and even complained that no one had thought to film the wolves as they charged up the mound. Filming continued after a guard from the manor came over with a sporting rifle to protect them from the escaped wolf if it returned.

"I hope the poor wolf doesn't get shot," said Melody. "It's not its fault it was set loose by some idiot."

"Don't worry," said Davy. "A wolf on its own won't come near a crowd of people. I just hope we can catch it before it attacks a sheep and gets shot by a crofter."

"Won't your people be in danger from the wolf?" Carol asked this with an eagerness that made you think she hoped they might be.

"I'll make sure everyone's in groups of at least three people and they keep in radio contact at all times. Nobody will be allowed to go off on their own. I think the wolf will keep to covered areas, like the woods. A single wolf is only dangerous if it's really hungry or frightened. Then it can become ferocious."

Extra film work had to be done to make up for the time lost to the wolves but Oswald rescheduled things so that the children's scenes were done first, as they were due to have the afternoon off.

After a late lunch Iain, Melody and Carol wandered round to the old stables at the back of the manor. No longer used, they were now acting as storerooms for props and costumes. Here was the little workshop that Harry shared with his colleague, Joe Phillips. The children told him the whole story as he had only heard a bare outline of what had happened.

"I hope he'll be better soon… but it leaves me with double the work to do. I've been working late to try to catch up."

"Look," said Melody, holding out the necklace Harry had given her. "Do you recognise this? We thought it might be one of your props."

Joe glanced at it. An anxious look flickered across his face.

"Where did you find it?"

"Harry gave it to me. He seemed really worried about it – so I took it rather than upset him."

"We thought it might be Ronnie's," said Carol. "She asked him to fix a necklace for her. But we've not been able to ask her about it."

"Oh? I didn't know. Leave it on Harry's worktable. It will be safe here. I always lock this room after work."

Melody put the necklace back in its little container. Joe had seemed to stare at it in a strange way.

"I think I'll keep it for now. We might get to see Ronnie today anyway." She gave a little gasp and put a hand to her mouth. "I've just had a thought. We ought to visit Harry and see how he is. Would you like us to give him a message?"

"You don't know Harry; why do you want to visit him?"

Melody looked a little hurt that she should be asked that question.

"He's one of us," she said, "even if he's not actually involved in the filming. All of you are important: props, dressers, makeup people and all the rest. We couldn't make the film without you."

Joe, whose mood had seemed to turn sour, beamed a smile at Melody.

"Bless you, child. Go ahead and visit him." His voice turned mock serious. "Tell him from me not to milk it. The work's piling up here."

They were turning to go, when Joe spoke again, this time in a very serious voice.

"Look, I think it would be a good idea if you said nothing about that necklace until after you've seen Harry."

The children all managed to show the exact same puzzled expression at the exact same time. They even asked the same one-word question together.

"Why?"

"I can't say, but if you really care about Harry please do as I ask."

They tried to get him to explain but he just shook his head, shrugged or grunted in answer. This was very frustrating and losing patience, Iain blurted out:

"Did Harry know the men who attacked him?"

He could have bitten his tongue off. What a stupid thing to say! Yet it got a response from Joe where their other questions had not.

"What are you trying to say?" His voice was loud and angry. "If Harry knew some crooks, then he could be a crook himself? That the attack was a falling out between crooks? You've got a nerve!"

They were all shocked at Joe's reaction. They had never thought this at all – not even Iain who had just spoke without thinking. They were red-faced and tongue-tied. Seeing their miserable faces, Joe calmed down and, shaking his head, told them,

"I'm sorry, kids. Lost my head there. Thing is, you touched a nerve with what you said. I've known Harry for a long time – we were good friends once. Then he got into trouble gambling and lost a lot of money. Some of the people he gambled with were crooks and they made him do some work for them to pay off his debt."

"You mean Harry helped them to rob people?" Melody looked shocked.

"No, of course not. But crooks who steal jewellery like to get someone like Harry to remake it so it looks different and they can sell it without it being recognised as stolen goods."

"Then Harry got caught?" Carol said. "I mean he must have or you wouldn't have known about this."

"Yes, you're right," said Joe, giving her a sharp

look. "But since it was his first offence and he gave evidence against the crooks, he got a light sentence. He found it hard getting work afterwards, so I helped him get a job here."

"Oh!" said Melody. "Maybe *that* was why these men attacked him – maybe they're the crooks he gave evidence against."

Joe chewed thoughtfully at the end of a drill bit he had been trying to fix into a miniature drill.

"I hadn't thought of that. That might be it. Poor Harry. Still, now they've had their revenge, maybe they'll leave him alone."

"Yes," said Iain, getting his confidence back, "and we can identify them. Or at least one of them."

"We described him to the police," added Melody.

Joe became serious again.

"Look, you watch out for yourselves. These are bad men and they don't mind using violence. I suppose they won't want to hang about a quiet place like this – the police would spot them too easily – but you never know." His manner became confidential. "Look here, Harry's a decent cove. Keep what I told you about him to yourselves. He needs his job here."

They nodded and promised they would do that.

"I know what it's like when someone spreads stories about you," said Melody. "We'll talk to Harry first before we say or do anything."

They went off to the break room where they had some tea and scones while they discussed what they had found out.

"Well, now we know that Harry was involved with these crooks," said Carol.

"Yes, but he didn't want to be," said Melody. "They'll maybe leave him alone now. They must know we'll have given their descriptions to the police."

"Just the one of them," said Iain. "We got a good look at him but only a glimpse of the other man. He looked very ordinary."

"I wonder about that necklace though," said Carol. "Remember that car that nearly knocked you down, Iain? You said it might be going to… what was it?"

"*An Sloc Beag*," said Iain. "I bet you're thinking they were crooks, going to spy out houses out for a burglary."

"Well, we know now they *are* crooks. Maybe they stole the necklace there and finding out Harry was here, gave it to him to alter it for them?"

"Why would they attack him if he agreed?" asked Melody. "They weren't acting like he was working with them. How could they expect him to help them if he was in hospital?"

"Well…" began Carol but Iain interrupted.

"Stop arguing about it! We just don't know. We promised not to say anything to anyone else, so we'll just have to wait."

"Until we've spoken to Harry again," said Carol.

"Maybe we should go and see him this evening. He might be able to tell us what it was really all about."

"We had better phone the hospital first to check if he's well enough to have visitors," said Iain.

Melody got up. "Good idea. I'll do that now."

She went off to find one of the manor's landline telephones. As she went, Iain sat up, both eyes and mouth wide open.

"Oh! I forgot – I promised Raj and Raveena I'd ask if they could visit us on set here."

"We all did. It's just that discovering the necklace put it right out of our minds – and we had that early start this morning then all those wolves."

"I suppose so." Iain grinned. "Raj will be annoyed he missed the wolves. It was like something in those fantasy computer games he plays."

"Only real, not computer graphics. We'll look for Oswald when Mel gets back and arrange that visit for your friends."

"We'll have to wait till tomorrow to see Harry," Melody told them. "We can go in the afternoon or early evening. We'll decide when we know our filming schedule."

It didn't take long for them to find out because Oswald was looking for them. He had scripts for the next day's shooting.

"You can have a lie in tomorrow – but not too long. You have to read these before your afternoon shooting starts. We're filming at the Barn studio so you won't bothered by any wild animals this time."

"Except for you, Oswald!" Carol laughed. "You can be wilder than a whole pack of wolves when you're upset."

Even Oswald cracked a little smile at this, although the joke was on him. Seeing this, Iain took the opportunity to ask about having the Akashs over to watch the filming. He agreed.

"That should be fine. Make sure they know what the rules are, though – keeping still and not making a sound while we're filming."

Iain shot off to phone Raj at his aunt's home. Ten minutes later he was back, looking thoughtful.

"I couldn't get hold of Raj but his aunt was in. She said she'd be glad to get rid of them for a while. She's going to bring them over this evening." Iain hesitated a moment. "She's expecting them to stay overnight... in fact I've a feeling she expects them to be staying for a few days."

"Well, why not?" said Carol. "Mel and I have a large bedroom and it's got a spare bed – Raveena could share with us."

"Raj can't share with me. My room is tiny and there's only one single bed. He'll have to go miles along the corridor to the old servant's room."

"We could drag the mattress and blankets from it into your room," said Carol, "and we could all be close together."

"Well, see what he prefers when he arrives."

The next thing to do was arrange passes for their friends, so they would be free to roam about. They sought out Jamie, the caretaker, who was in charge of this. He raised an eyebrow but gave them two passes anyway.

"These passes will do three days but if they get up to any mischief they'll be rescinded."

"They'll be with us most of the time," said Iain, "so they'll not get into any trouble."

Jamie flung his head back and laughed so hard that his shoulders shook.

"Not get into trouble… ha ha ha… with you three… ha ha ha…"

"What's so funny about that?" asked Carol, frowning.

"Nothing, really. Getting chased by apes? Fighting off wolves? Trouble? Of course not. If I see you sitting on an elephant charging through the manor, I'll know it's nothing to worry about. You never get into any trouble."

Jamie roared with laughter but they had their passes so they went off quickly before they were tempted to say something rude and have them rescinded before the Akashs could use them. It was getting close to dinner time anyway.

After dinner, they felt too full to do anything energetic, so they sat in the break room and read their scripts.

Oswald had some of the cast filming late into the evening, so it was relatively quiet. Before they could get too bored, however, one of the manor staff came in and told them,

"A Mrs Akash is at the gate – says her kids are here to visit you."

They all leapt from their chairs, scattering scripts all over the floor.

"*Tha mi gòrach*," said Iain. "I'm an idiot! I should have fixed a definite time to meet them. Now we'll have to run like mad."

"Or use our bikes," said Melody.

"No, we won't," said Carol. "Follow me!"

They hurried out and Carol led them to the back of the house.

"How does this help?" asked Iain. "We're going away from the main gate."

Carol laughed and pointed over to the grassy sward that swept around the manor.

"Come on," she said, and ran off to where the groundskeepers had been working earlier. Old Cromarty was there, sitting on one of two small motorised carts. They looked a little bit like golf carts but were used to get about the large manor grounds and carry tools and equipment to wherever they were needed. Carol jumped on to the other cart and told Iain and her sister:

"Hurry, get on." She turned to the old gardener. "You don't mind if we borrow this, do you, Crom?"

Without waiting for a reply and giving her friends barely time to get on the cart, she pressed the accelerator with her foot and the cart shot off. Luckily, the carts were very simple to operate. Carol drove them quickly back the way they had come. Old Cromarty shook his fist at them, but they were sure he didn't mind. He still had one cart to sit in and smoke his pipe.

They found a kind of silly thrill motoring down at top speed to the gate.

"The good thing about this," said Carol, "is that Raj and Raveena can squeeze in with us coming back."

As luck would have it, they saw their friends right away beside two guards. Their aunt was with them but stood well back from the gate. Raj and Raveena were dressed in their best clothes but with bulging packs on their backs. They were kneeling down, petting a guard dog which seemed a mixture of Alsatian and some other breed. They both looked up when the cart trundled up to them. The dog barked and Raj and his sister ran over to them. They all high-fived each other and Raveena gave everyone a hug for good measure. Aunt Nyra came over, wearing an ordinary, plain dress but with a bright orange headscarf covering her head and shoulders.

"Right, you two," she said, "behave yourselves – and phone me each day so I know you're OK."

Her rough manner faded for a moment as she bent over to give them both a kiss. Then with a final warning about their behaviour, she got in her car and drove off. The guard dog gave a friendly bark as if it was saying *goodbye!* Iain went over to pat it.

"This is new," he said. "We didn't have guard dogs before."

"It's because of the fence cutting," said the female guard who held the dog's leash. "The Laird has ordered extra security."

"He's very friendly for a guard dog," said Carol. "Would he be just as friendly to intruders?"

"*He's* a *she*," said the guard. "Sasha's her name. She senses I'm comfortable with you, so she accepts you as friends. Besides, she's well trained – if she saw an intruder, she'd grab their trouser bottom or jacket sleeve. Unless the intruder became violent towards me, then she'd do more than that."

"She's lovely," said Melody. "Is she part Husky?"

"Well spotted. Yes, she is. She'll know you now and be friendly – but don't get up to any nonsense in the grounds or I'll have to set her on you!" But she said this with a grin. "I'm Bobbie, by the way. If you'd like to see Sasha again, ask for Bobbie Milne – but only when we're off duty."

Raj and Raveena flung their backpacks into the cart and squeezed in beside their friends. They shot off again, turned sharply and rushed over the enormous lawn back towards the manor.

They went first to their bedrooms so the Akashs could dump their luggage. As Carol had thought, Raj preferred to share a bedroom and they had a rumbustious time raiding the unused bedroom for a mattress, pillows and sheets.

When they were finished, Raj tried out his bed by flinging himself down and bouncing a few times on it.

"Brilliant! This mattress is really thick and bouncy. I'll sleep well on it."

"Will you show us around?" asked Raveena. "There must be tons to see."

"Yeah, and maybe we could get a snack as well," said her brother.

Raveena leaned over and ruffled his hair, laughing.

"You must be starving – it's nearly an hour since we had dinner."

"You're right." Raj ignored the sarcasm. "I need more than a snack."

They set off and had just got halfway down the stairs between the second and first floors when they heard an anguished cry.

NINE

WE'VE BEEN BURGLED

The first floor was where the adult actors were living, in large and beautifully decorated rooms. Here, Ronnie Mere, Ravi Ansari, Martin Trout, Susie Reynard and a few others stayed – as did Oswald Wales who was in his own way a star, though he seldom acted these days.

The children rushed down and almost ran into Susie who was hurrying along the corridor.

"Susie! What's up?" Melody looked past her and along the corridor as she spoke. She saw the door to her bedroom was wide open.

Susie was furious and for a moment the children thought she was going to start shouting at them. But she took a deep breath and calmed herself down. She gazed, puzzled for a moment to see the Akashs. Then she saw their passes and realised they were the other children's guests. When she spoke there was a cold anger in her voice.

"Someone's been in my room and they've been rummaging through my stuff. My room's a complete mess."

"Was anything stolen?" Carol's tone was a combination of sympathy and eager curiosity.

"Just some money I left on my dresser. That's not important. It's the fact that someone has been going through all my belongings, looking at all my personal stuff. It just makes my skin crawl."

"Have you checked all your valuables?" asked Raj. "I mean, thieves will steal things they can sell, as well as money."

"I wonder if the thief has been in any other rooms," said Melody.

"You're right," said Carol. "Let's check them."

She rushed off and began to check the doors. Susie watched her, amused but thoughtful.

"You've got me thinking," she said. "There are things that can be valuable which you wouldn't think were worth anything at first."

She disappeared into her room. The other children joined Carol in checking the doors. They were all locked except Martin Trout's room. The door swung open at a push and they looked in.

"Martin? Are you there?" This was Carol.

There was no answer, so they went in.

"Wow! This is a mess too," said Iain.

"Maybe," said Raj, "this is how it always looks. Some people are untidy, you know."

"Don't be so daft," said Raveena. "Look at all these cupboard doors and drawers left wide open and the clothes falling out of them. Someone's been searching through them."

They suddenly sensed someone behind them and turned to see Susie staring into the room. Her face was a picture of absolute fury.

"So, Martin has been burgled too. First Harry and now this. What a mess they've made! When they catch whoever did this, I'd like them to give me five minutes alone with them. I'd make a mess of *them*!"

She stormed off, muttering vague threats to herself about what she would like to do to the burglar.

The children looked at each other, smothering laughter with their hands. As soon as Susie was out of sight – and hearing – they fell together letting howls of laughter ring along the corridor.

"You can just see Susie beating up these two thugs, can't you?" said Carol, gasping for breath.

Susie was only a little taller than the children themselves and was slim and light. The picture of her fighting a big strong man made them all laugh again. Eventually they stopped and Melody said,

"That's all very well, but it's really quite serious. We'll have to tell the police that Baldy and his pal have burgled our manor."

"No," said Iain. "We don't know for sure they did it. And there's something funny about this. Baldy and his pal must be *professional* jewel thieves. I can't see them bothering to steal stuff worth so little – or making such a mess."

"Jewel thieves!" Raj and Raveena cried out together. Raj asked, "How do you know that?"

"We'll tell you later," said Melody. "It's quite a story. But you have to keep it a secret for now."

Their eyes glinted at the thought of a secret involving jewel thieves. Carol now thought of something.

"What about the other rooms? Susie and Martin left their doors unlocked and some others could be unlocked too. I think we should see if any other rooms were burgled. It will take a while for the police to get here anyway."

"We could check the rooms on the next floor," said Iain. "The other ones here are locked."

"Let's check them!" said Raj, eager to catch up on what he'd missed of the adventure. Iain and Carol led the way upstairs but they were to be disappointed. All the rooms were locked except for one and that was occupied by three of the camera crew. They were playing cards and were quite astonished when the children burst in. Luckily they were more amused than annoyed. They were much more interested in returning to their card game than doing anything about the burglary when they were told about it.

"Sorry to bother you," said Melody, as they left.

They went back down just in time to meet Susie who had returned with Martin and Oswald. Martin brushed past them and into his room. A moment later there was a terrific shout followed by a string of swear words.

"You kids get back to your rooms," said Susie. "This isn't any business of yours."

"It's all right," said Carol. "We've heard far worse language from you when you've lost your temper."

She ducked and skipped away laughing as Susie swung a mock punch at her. The others followed and they ran upstairs. However, they stopped at the landing and leaned over, listening as hard as they could. At first they couldn't make out what was said. Soon, the voices became clearer.

"Well, at least nothing valuable was stolen." This was Oswald's loud, rumbling voice.

"That depends what you mean by valuable." Susie sounded worried. "Some of my personal things are missing – my diary and some photographs."

The next voice was Martin's. "I've nothing really personal with me but my notebooks have been searched and a computer memory stick is missing.

It just had notes on local history – it's a hobby of mine."

"Well," said Oswald. "The police will be here soon and you can tell them what's happened. I'll speak to the other cast members and get them to check their rooms just in case."

Their voices faded and then disappeared as they went down the stairs. The children went upstairs and gathered again in the bigger girl's room.

"All right," said Raj. "What's all this about jewel thieves?"

"We promised to keep it to ourselves for a while," said Carol. "So don't tell anyone."

"We can tell you because you're already involved," said Iain. "You were with us when Harry got attacked."

Carol, with fortunately few interruptions, told them what they had found out about Harry's past. Raveena insisted on seeing the necklace, so Melody took it out from its hiding place under her mattress. On a whim, she hung it on her neck, its green, red and white precious stones glittering in the lamplight. Raveena gasped and ran her fingers over the jewels.

"Ooooh! It's gorgeous! Look at these emeralds… and these must be rubies… and diamonds. It must be worth a fortune."

"If it's real," said Raj. "It might just be something Harry was working on for the movie."

"Joe would have known if it was," said Carol. "It

might be Ronnie's though, so we have to find out."

"Well, until we know for sure we'd better hide it," said Melody, "and we'll keep it to ourselves until we can ask Harry about it."

"Of course," said Raj. "We promised, didn't we?" He rubbed his stomach and groaned. "I'm really hungry now. Where can I get a snack?"

Raveena groaned.

"We should have dragged your mattress down to the kitchen, wherever that is, and left you there."

"I'll show you," said Carol. She got up so eagerly, the others suspected an ulterior motive and there was one. "There's a way out to the back from the kitchen. We could sneak out and have a look around for clues as to how the burglar got in."

"I suppose so," said Melody, doubtfully. "But we've already got one mystery to investigate, can we really manage another one?"

"We can't do anything about the jewel mystery until tomorrow," said Iain. "So why not do this now? Besides, it was rude how Susie and the rest chased us off as if we'd just get in the way. If we could find a clue it would show them how wrong they were."

"Yeah," said Carol, "after all, we saved the day when the wolves attacked."

"Wolves!" cried Raj and Raveena together.

So the expedition was put off for a little while as they told the story of the morning's adventure to their friends.

"Super-wowie-fantastic!" cried Raveena, jumping up and down on her bed.

"Don't let us miss out on any more excitement, will you?" said Raj. "Now, how about that search for clues."

They collected torches and set off. They could hear loud voices from below as they went towards the rear of the house. The noise faded as they slipped down the backstairs – down and down until they came to the basement. This was where most of the servants lived and worked in the old days when the manor could afford to keep dozens of servants. Nowadays there were only two maids, the caretaker, a cook, and some part-time staff. However, the kitchen was down here and from the kitchen there was a door that led out of the house.

"Can we stop long enough to grab a bite to eat?" asked Raj, looking worried. "I enjoy a mystery but I work best on a full stomach."

"This is enormous," said Raveena, looking round the kitchen as she went to the back door. "Oh, it's locked."

Beside the door was a row of small hooks, each with a key hanging from it. Carol tried three keys before she found the right one. Then they went out and climbed the short flight of stairs to the back area.

"You know," said Carol, "the burglar might have tried to break into the workshops too. Let's check that first."

They ran across to the narrow alley that led to the storehouses and workshops, used by the film crew. Everything was quite dim here now where buildings or walls enclosed each side. With their torches lighting their way, they walked over and examined all the doors and windows carefully. No light could be seen in any of the workshops; everything was dark and every door was locked.

"Well, that's that," said Carol. "Nobody's tried to break in here. Let's go round the grounds and see if we can find any clues."

They walked to the end of the narrow passage and out round to the west wing of the manor house. The sun was setting but on this side of the building there was still some light – a soft, fading light but still light enough to see by.

"Look," said Raj, "something's been dragged along the grass there."

"Yes," said Melody, bending her neck to see better. "I see it now. What made the mark? A wheelbarrow? Do you think the burglar maybe made off with the stolen goods in it?"

"Don't be daft," said Carol. "He didn't steal anything like enough stuff to need a wheelbarrow. Iain, did you ever hear such nonsense?"

But Iain wasn't there. He was running across the grass towards the bushes that marked the limit of the inner grounds of the manor. The other four ran after him, Raj complaining all the time about running on an empty stomach. Iain pointed to a part of the house where a column of windows glittered between several half-towers that stuck out from the wall. It was these tower-like projections which gave the manor it its castle-like appearance.

"See! Nobody could see a burglar climbing in – except from where we're standing now – and nobody comes to this area much."

They walked over and stared up at the windows. There were no ground floor windows here as there were at the front: a ladder was needed if you wanted to reach any of them.

"Look," said Carol, "all the first-floor windows are barred. We've been here for weeks and I didn't notice."

"Well, we never really came round to this side of the manor much," said Melody.

"Anyway, no one could get in from this side without an enormous ladder. Let's try round this way."

There was no sign of anything that way either.

"I've looked carefully at the ground just below the windows," said Raj, "and there wasn't any sign of footprints or marks that might have been made by a ladder."

"Do you think they might have been able to sneak in the front way?" asked Melody. "Maybe pretending they had business here?"

"No way!" said Carol. "There are too many

people about; besides there are security guards at the main door all the time. They wouldn't let any strangers pass without questioning them."

Iain shook his head and frowned as he tried to work out the problem.

"It's a real mystery. We know a burglar got in but there doesn't seem to be any way he *could* have got in."

TEN

FOLLOWING TRAILS

They all felt somewhat down. They had thought they would find clues or at least see how the burglar had broken in.

"Let's just wander about a bit before we go back," said Carol. "You never know, we might spot something."

They wandered around and soon found themselves in a pleasant little orchard surrounded by a large hedge. And here, by luck, they at last found a clue.

"Look here," said Iain. "You can just see footprints… somebody walked behind the hedges here. He kept close to them… so he must have been trying to keep out of sight."

"So, he couldn't be seen from the manor windows," said Raj. "Come on, let's follow and see where they lead."

The prints were sometimes little more than slight indentations in the grass, sometimes a little clearer where the ground was soft. Here and there in a little muddy patch the mark of a boot stood out sharply. They followed, careful to avoid treading on the trail, until after walking a couple of hundred metres it led them into a little, run-down garden. The entrance to it was overgrown so that it was half hidden and they only found the way in because they were following the footprints.

"This must be the Ladywell garden," said Iain. The others gave him a surprised look. "I may not have stayed here before, but I've read their tourist booklets."

He pointed to the centre of the garden – which was surrounded by bushes and hedges – where what looked like a miniature Roman temple stood.

"Great gooseberries," said Carol. "I never knew this was here."

Its stone columns were dull and pitted with age and overgrown with weeds and moss. Inside the narrow circle of the columns were two small statues on a low dais, very old and stained and covered with moss.

"There was an old well here long ago," explained Iain, "called 'the Lady well'."

"So they built the garden round it?"

"Yes. I think that was way back in the eighteenth century."

"But where's the well now?"

"Under the statues – if it's still there. You see, a previous Laird's young son climbed up for a dare and fell in. After that they covered it over and built this thing – I think they call it a folly – over it."

"Did the boy die?"

"Yes. It's a bit sad that it's been allowed to go to ruin like this."

"Well, the ground is all hard here," said Raj. "So no footprints."

"Maybe, but there's lots of weeds here, and look, you can see where someone has broken the stalks walking through."

They followed the new trail and it led… into the folly. They looked around it – it didn't take long for the folly wasn't very big – and they found nothing. At least they found nothing to show where the intruder had gone.

"The moss is scuffed and scraped over here," said Carol. "But where can he have gone? This thing is completely surrounded by weeds and wildflowers but there's only the trail coming here. There's no sign of anyone going away from here."

"Maybe he walked very carefully," said Raj. He wasn't sure about this himself. It seemed unlikely but what other explanation could there be?

Iain began crawling around the folly, examining the stone flags on which the statues stood. He had the beginning of an idea and might have found out something then, but Carol suddenly said,

"Look, let's go back to where we saw the muddy footprints. I've got my mobile with me – we can use its camera to photograph them."

So back they went, running now by the light of their torches as it was getting dark. They found the footprints.

"The best one's here," said Melody, pointing to a muddy patch. "Wait! I'll put this pencil beside it. It will let us judge the size in the photograph."

"Take a photo of this one, too," said Iain. "It's not as good a print but there's a corner that's clear which is missing from the other one."

"Good idea," said Raj, as Carol's camera flashed. "I can use the two pictures to make a complete picture of the footprint on my computer."

Carol grinned as she took the second photograph. She felt like she was doing some real detective work at last.

"Let's see if there's any footprints we missed before."

They searched around until they reached a spot near a wooded area, which edged one side of the manor. Here the grass was so short and the ground so hard that it was impossible to see any prints.

"Well, that's that," said Iain. "The man must have come in through the wood and walked round into the garden."

"Why?"

"He might have been spying out the land, then hid in the garden for a bit. Or maybe he saw some folk about."

"Yes, but if he was our burglar," said Melody, "how on earth did he get into the house? He couldn't have climbed in – we saw the ground back there would have left marks."

"It's a mystery. I'm really tired now; let's go back."

They made their way back round the manor, still using their torches until they were approaching the back door once again. They were chattering away when suddenly there was a loud bark followed by low growling.

"The wolf!" cried Melody, thinking of the wolf that had escaped that morning and was still missing. But it wasn't.

"Sasha!" Raveena shouted first but the others repeated the name.

"Easy, lass," said a voice. Bobbie Milne appeared in the light of their torches, flashing her own in their faces.

"What are you lot doing out here at this time of night?"

Five voices answered at once – and Sasha barked an accompaniment – from which Bobbie could only distinguish the words *burglary, clues* and *searching.*

"Daft gowks!" she called them. "If there had been a burglar out here, what could you have done?" She shook her head. "Get back indoors and lock that door. Or I'll set my dog on you."

The last seemed unlikely as Sasha had decided they were all to be good friends and was licking their hands. They did go in as they had done all they could do for now.

When they were back inside the house, they discovered that Detective Sergeant Innes and PC Cowan had arrived from Ardriagh and were interviewing Susie and Martin. They headed over towards the little group but Oswald, the film director came over and blocked their way.

"This is no concern of yours: just go up to bed now and get some rest. You've got important scenes to do tomorrow."

"But we've found—" began Carol.

"No arguments," Oswald said, pushing them back. "Off to your beds!"

He just would not listen to them so finally they gave up and made their way upstairs, muttering to themselves.

"I suppose the police will find the same things we did," said Iain. "I mean it's their job, isn't it?"

"For goodness' sake," said Carol. "We've a right to investigate ourselves. They needn't be so rude; besides the police might not find our clues."

"We should make a casebook or something," said Iain, "and record all our evidence in it."

"I don't see how it will help," said Melody. "There wasn't any clue as to how the burglars got in."

"Well, it must mean something," said Carol. "The footprints must belong to the burglars. Nobody else would have gone into the Ladywell garden; we saw how overgrown it is."

"I'll do it," said Raj. "If we put down everything we know, it might help us get some ideas later."

It was very late now and it had been a very busy day so they went back upstairs. Raj unpacked and set up a small laptop. In ten minutes, he had loaded the photographs they'd taken and merged the two partial footprint images into one clear single image of a complete footprint.

"Wow!" said Carol. "It would have taken me ages to do that."

"I measured Mel's pencil and worked out a rough size of the boot. It's a size twelve. The depth of the muddy print makes it likely he's a heavy man."

"Terrific! Smart work, Raj."

Raj began typing up a summary of the events they had witnessed separately or together. Everyone talked at once to say what they thought or saw. So he covered his ears.

"STOP! Stop talking at once, please. Melody, you describe Baldy – you saw him twice."

Raj got it done much quicker after that; the others were amazed at the speed at which he typed. Once it was done, they stared at the screen, wondering.

"It doesn't seem so much when you write it down like that," said Melody.

"I've only put down the facts that we know – I've left out theories and speculation."

"Are they all connected?" asked Iain. "Or are they separate? Or are some of them connected and the others aren't?"

But they couldn't make anything out of it; they didn't have enough information yet. Raj shook his head and closed his laptop.

"All this concentration has made me hungry."

They all laughed at this – and laughed even more when he produced a packet of biscuits. Soon, they were all yawning. In their separate bedrooms they dragged on pyjamas and fell into bed, their sleep accompanied by dreams of wolves, burglars, huge apes and a dark, haunted broch.

They had a long lie in the next day and didn't get up until nearly 9.30 am. Or at least it was a long lie to the three young actors, who usually had to start filming much earlier.

"These are the school holidays," complained Raj as Iain shook him. "I usually don't get up until eleven o'clock."

"How do you survive without breakfast?" joked Iain. "Or are you like a bear hibernating in winter?"

Raj groaned beneath his sheets. He didn't want to move but the mention of breakfast put images of all kinds of food into his brain. He dragged himself up and washed his face in the little handbasin in their room. Then, dressed in shorts and his moon-themed T-shirt, he staggered downstairs. The girls were already in the dining room, halfway through toast and scrambled eggs and bacon. It didn't take the boys long to catch up and for once all five were silent as they concentrated on eating.

Afterwards they split up. The three young actors had to go over their scripts, so Raj and Raveena were left to their own devices. Raveena went off to explore the great manor. She took her mobile with her as well as her autograph book, hoping to run into some of the actors and get their pictures and autographs. All the actors she would have recognised were either filming or rehearsing so she had no luck. She didn't mind though. There were still a few of the film people about who, responding to her bubbly personality, chatted with her about the making of the film.

Raj spent most of the morning on his computer. He had intended to do some internet searches to help with their mystery but ended up playing an online game of *Dragons and Danger*. He got so engrossed he nearly missed lunch and almost bowled over his sister on the way to the dining room. Their actor friends had already eaten and had gone off to get costumed and made up. They ate quickly then went to see them performing.

Filming had started but the Akashs couldn't see their friends. The studio was so dim that the only thing they could see clearly was the huge screen, glowing a bright blue. They were gradually able to make out a rather theatrical set up of the top of a castle tower. It looked quite artificial at first, as if it was made of painted cardboard. The next moment, just as they settled in at the back behind the cameras, the lighting technician flipped switches and different coloured lights beamed out. Suddenly everything looked very real, in fact almost more real than real.

"Look! There's Iain. Doesn't he look funny dressed up like that? Look at his ears!"

Raveena didn't speak very loudly but a man wearing big earphones turned round and told them to be quiet.

"Otherwise," he said, "you'll have to leave."

Raj giggled when a young woman began to powder Iain's face but after a sharp dig in the ribs from Raveena, he made no other sound. Martin Trout appeared, dressed in his wizard costume; a false moustache and beard gave his normally pleasant face a rather sinister appearance. Iain now stood atop the highest part of the 'tower', holding a gleaming white staff in his hand. A boom with a large microphone at its end swung over the two actors. Two big cameras, from different angles, moved in towards them and various crew members moved out of shot to peer over banks of instruments or stand and watch. Oswald, the director, stood beside the nearest camera operator and shouted out:

"Quiet everybody! Action!"

Iain and Martin had been standing, looking at nothing in particular; looking in fact just like a boy and a man dressed up in fancy costumes. As soon as Oswald shouted *Action!* they instantly took on poses and their expressions became alive. Their voices rang out over the set as they moved around like two fencers looking for an opening. They lifted their staffs and thrust them at each other as they moved. Raveena was puzzled by this until her brother whispered to her that special effects would be added later to make it look like they were shooting bursts of energy at each other.

"Cut!" Oswald went forward and shook Martin's hand. "That was very good. Well done, both of you, that was perfect, it's a *single* take[2]. Now we'll do some close-ups. You first, Martin. Iain, we'll need you for reaction while Martin does his lines."

---

2   When a scene is shot in a film it is called a take. Film makers often need several 'takes' to film a scene just right but occasionally it goes perfectly first time and this is called a 'single-take'.

Since the crew were all moving around and talking to each other, Raj thought it would be OK to quietly ask one of them,

"What does he mean, *reaction*?"

"The camera will only be filming Martin, really close up. He could do it just by himself, but most actors prefer to have another actor facing them and *reacting* to what they say rather than just talking to empty space. It helps them get their performance right."

What he said next was drowned out by a shout of,

"Places everybody! Silence on the set!" and then, "Action!" as they began filming the close ups.

After this, Iain and Martin went away and another actor named Wendy Forester appeared, made up as a rather hideous witch. Melody and Carol followed and they ran through another scene, involving just the three of them.

Other scenes followed as the afternoon wore on, some with all of their friends appearing together. Very often scenes in films have to be done over and over again so that even short sequences of a film can take a long time to complete. However, on rare occasions, everything will go perfectly and it all gets done very quickly. This was one of these exceptional occasions when everything went smoothly and well. So much so that Raj and Raveena were surprised to find how quickly the afternoon had passed. They were allowed to come and chat with their friends as they got changed and their make-up removed. As her wig was removed, Melody glanced at her watch.

"If we're going to visit Harry, we'd better hurry. There's no time for more than a quick snack before we go."

"It's not healthy to go without proper meals," complained Raj.

"We can get proper meals in town," Raveena told him. "But we need to catch the next bus. We'll miss it if we don't get a move on, and there's not so many buses in the evening. There's no time for a snack first."

"Oh, no!" cried Raj, horrified.

ELEVEN

SUSPICIOUS CHARACTERS

They tumbled out of the bus and walked briskly along the main road, peering into various shop windows.

"We need to get something for Harry," said Melody, "and it's best to do it now so we don't have to rush later."

"Don't be all day," said Carol. "It's still the tourist season and the shops will be busy."

"Try this place," said Iain, pointing at a little gift shop at the corner of the street.

They trooped in, peering round at greetings cards and boxes of chocolates. Melody bought a get-well card and a box of chocolates with soft centres.

"Harry might not be able to eat anything you need to really bite into," she said.

"Would you like these wrapped?" the shop assistant asked.

"Yes, please," said Melody.

They bought some fruit in a nearby grocers and then, as they were all feeling hungry now, they quickly found a little café and ordered pizzas. They had just sat down at an outdoor table to wait for their order, when Iain said,

"Oh, no! Look who's coming."

"Slippery snakes!" said Raj. "It's the Weasel. I hope he doesn't notice us."

Melody and Carol put their heads down and pretended to read the menu. But perhaps he had spotted Iain, for he came up and stood by their table. He gave them a grin which reminded them of a slobbering hyena. He brought out a notepad and pencil, which the twins thought strange. In their experience, reporters nowadays just recorded you on their mobiles.

"We're not allowed to talk about the film or any of the actors," said Carol, scowling at him.

"We're not going to talk about the WFF either," said Iain. He wanted to protect his friends. The Weasel laughed.

"I've plenty of material on all that! My name's Dan Wissall, by the way – here's my card." He dropped a grubby-looking card on their table. "No, everyone knows about that. I'm more interested in the assault you witnessed."

"Why do you want to know about that?" Iain was curious, despite not liking the man. "How do you know about it?"

"I'm a reporter, it's my job to find out these things. It's a story nobody else bothered about – so they don't know that three young film stars were involved." He gave Iain a wink at this. "The man assaulted was one of the film crew. Do you know him? Can you tell me what the attackers looked like?"

"All that must be in the police report," said Carol, eyeing him suspiciously. "Why are you bothering us?"

"Police reports don't tell you everything. Anything unusual you saw or heard could make a good story. Some quotes would be good, too. How about something on the Laird claiming the WFF are behind the burglary?"

For a moment they were all too shocked to speak. Had the Laird actually accused their friends of a new crime? However, they didn't want to give the reporter the satisfaction of a reply to this.

"I'll give you a quote," said Carol. The reporter's eyes gleamed, his pencil poised over his notepad. "NO COMMENT!"

The Weasel winced. At that moment, their pizza order arrived. They got up and walked off, delving deep into their pizzas. The Weasel followed them for a few minutes but, seeing they were keeping their mouths full of pizza and would be giving him no answers, he gave up.

"Pest of a man," said Melody. "I was worried he might follow us all the way to the hospital."

"Oh no!" said Iain. "Do you think he might pester Harry?"

"Jumping giraffes!" said Carol. "Imagine if Harry's story got out, about how he used to be involved with crooks. He might lose his job."

"I knew that Weasel would be trouble the moment I heard about him," said Melody. "I wouldn't be surprised if he had something to do with the thefts at the manor. Like that reporter who stole personal stuff to get a story."

"Just as well we kept our lips zipped," said Raveena. "And stuffed with pizza."

By the time they finished their pizza, they were almost at the hospital.

The hospital had been a large mansion once and had been converted to replace the old 'cottage hospital' which the town had outgrown. They were making their way to Harry's ward when they heard shouting.

"Harry's in trouble!" said Iain, and he ran.

They all ran after him, for if there really was trouble, it wouldn't be good for Iain to meet it alone. When they reached the ward, they saw a nurse grasping a man by the arm and pointing towards the way out. He was a little taller than the nurse but slightly built, so he was finding it a struggle to push her away.

"If you don't leave now, I'll call security," she said.

In a flash of anger, he raised a fist as if to strike her – but he stopped when he saw five pairs of young eyes staring at him. His eyes grew large with astonishment.

"Bleedin' Norah! You lot again!"

He pushed the nurse away, burst past the children and shot off down the corridor and out of sight. The children were too surprised to say anything. The nurse wasn't.

"If you've come to visit Mr Puddock, I'm afraid you can't. That horrible man you just saw has upset him. He needs—"

"It's all right, Nurse." Harry's voice came from inside the ward. "I know them and I want to see them."

The nurse gave them a sour look, but stepped to one side.

"All right, but I'll be back in fifteen minutes to make sure they don't overstrain you. In you go – but behave yourselves."

They found Harry looking better, though far from fully recovered. He had a bandage on his head and his cuts and bruises were livid, though beginning to heal. They all looked at each other nervously. Would it be right to question Harry if he really was in a bad way?

"We brought you a present," said Melody. "Some soft-centre chocolates."

"And we brought a get-well card, too," said Raveena. "We all signed it."

Melody handed over a large envelope along with the box of chocolates.

"You seem to be looking better, now."

"That wouldn't be hard considering the state I was in when you last saw me."

"I suppose so," said Carol. "How do you feel?"

"A bit better," he said, surprising them with a broad grin. "But I'm seeing double." He laughed at his own joke about the twins. "Thanks for this. I think I can manage a few of these."

He tapped the lid of the chocolate box, opened it and popped a chocolate into his mouth then handed the box round.

"It would be rude to refuse," said Raj, grabbing two.

"Greedy pig!" said Raveena.

Nevertheless, she took one and so did the others.

"It's great to see you so cheerful," said Melody. "Will they let you out soon?"

"Joe said he'll expect you to do overtime to catch up with your work," said Carol. She grinned to show she wasn't serious. Harry laughed, a wheezing laugh which showed he still wasn't back to full health.

Melody had half pulled out the little case that held the necklace Harry had given her. Perhaps he glimpsed it, for he suddenly became serious, and said,

"Come here, close, and we'll speak quiet. I've something important to say."

They drew in as near as they could get, looking round at the other patients. It was a small ward that had six beds but only two others were occupied. In one, a young man sat up with headphones, listening to music; in the other, an elderly man lay back, apparently asleep.

"I know I can trust you, because you've still got that case I gave you – and besides, Joe phoned and let me know he'd told you about my old trouble."

They looked around but couldn't see a telephone. Harry laughed.

"He gave a nurse a message to pass on to me. It didn't say anything directly but he knew I'd understand."

"Like a code?" said Raj. Harry nodded with a smile.

"We all promised we would keep it secret," said Melody, "until we saw you and let you explain things."

Harry thought for a moment, then said,

"Well, I can cut a long story short. I gave evidence against those crooks and got off lightly. Unfortunately, they found I was working up here and—"

"They attacked you to get revenge?" Carol said.

"Not exactly… thing is they've been burgling houses in this area, with the help of some local crook. He tells them what places have really valuable stuff and when the owners will be away."

"Wow!" said Iain. "We didn't know of any robberies in this area."

"But we do!" said Raveena. "We were there when it happened."

"There was a burglary the other day at the manor," explained Melody. "Sue and Martin had some stuff stolen."

"But nothing valuable," added Iain. "It was an odd kind of burglary."

"Sorry to hear that," said Harry, "but it couldn't have been the men I was talking about... they're professionals. You wouldn't have heard what they've been up to because they've been breaking into houses where the family's been away for days or weeks on holiday. I know how they operate. Nobody will have discovered the burglaries yet."

"Did these men tell you all this?" asked Iain.

"Yes. You know the kind of work I do. They had a really valuable necklace and they wanted me to fix it, so it looked different. They threatened me and pushed it into my pocket, but I didn't want it. If I got caught helping them this time, I'd get a long prison sentence. But when I tried to give it back, they gave me a thumping and said they'd do worse if I didn't help them. They overdid it though and put me in here where I can't do anything for the moment. It doesn't look it, but it was a lucky break for me."

"Oh!" Melody glanced back at the other patients, but no one was paying attention to them. "We weren't sure before but that must mean that this is the stolen necklace."

She opened her little case and showed the necklace, carefully shielding it from other people's view with her body.

"Yes, it is. I'm sorry I dumped it on you. I didn't want the police to find it on me. It would have been jail for me for certain."

"We'll keep it a bit longer, if you like," said Carol. "It's not your fault these crooks forced it on you."

"Maybe not. But it's not safe for *you* to keep it – that thug you saw causing a ruckus was one of them. He was here to get the necklace back. They got carried away when they attacked me. They got too mad for revenge and forgot they needed me to fix it up. Things are hot for them now after you told the police what you saw. They wanted to be well away from here as soon as they got the necklace fixed – which I could have done yesterday if they hadn't put me in here."

"Well, they're bound to leave this area now," said Raj, "since we can identify two of them."

"No!" said Harry, very firmly. "That necklace is the most valuable thing they've ever stolen and they won't leave without it. You kids better watch yourselves – they know you can identify them."

"They can't get at us up at the manor," said Carol. "There are security guards."

"Well, keep away from the town for the next few

days. I'm not going to let you or any other people get into trouble on my account."

"But we want to help!"

"These villains are dangerous – I don't want you to have any more to do with this. The minute the doctor tells me I'm fit enough to leave here I'm going straight to the police. Give me the necklace. I'm sorry I was selfish enough to get you involved. I guess I wasn't thinking straight because of that bash on the head I got."

He held out his hand for the necklace case but at that moment the nurse came in and brusquely told them,

"That's your fifteen minutes up, you'll have to go now. Mr Puddock has had a trying time and needs to rest."

While she was fussing around her patient, Melody and Raveena huddled together, whispering. The others were complaining and asking the nurse to give them a few more minutes. Harry was anxious about the necklace.

"Nurse, these children were bringing me something I'd lost – let me have it, please."

"It can wait until later," she told him. Then, seeing his anxious expression, "Very well, I don't want you worrying about it. If they give it to me, I'll put it in your bedside locker with your other stuff. It will be safe there."

Melody handed over the case and the nurse

put it the locker drawer and turned the key. Harry waved them off. They were surprised to see that rather than worried or upset, he seemed relaxed and contented, as if a great weight had been lifted from him.

"I'll be all right," he said. "You lot be on your way; I've got to take my medicine now."

He laughed as if he had made a great joke. The nurse shooed them out and they went off, waving back to Harry.

As they went back down the corridor the nurse overtook them.

"Don't worry," she said. "I've warned the security people to be careful who they let in, so Mr Puddock won't be pestered again."

The nurse's rather dour expression vanished for a moment as she flashed a smile at the twins.

"You won't have trouble getting in – your faces are well known here. Your pictures are up on posters all over the town." She gave Iain an odd look. "Oh, and you, too. I didn't recognise you there without your elf's ears!"

With a little laugh, she went off, leaving them standing in the corridor. Raveena smothered a laugh.

"You do look cute as an elf – and even when you're not an elf."

She giggled and Iain felt his cheeks getting hot. Melody looked round and saw they were now alone.

"OK, Ravee," she said, "it's safe to show it now."

"Show what?" asked Carol. "What have you two been up to?"

Raveena lifted her T-shirt and pulled round the purple bum bag she was wearing. Opening it, she brought out and opened a case very like the one that had been handed over. She dangled from her fingers – the necklace!

"But you gave it to the nurse——"

"No, she didn't," said Raj, "they swapped it with something else while the nurse was seeing to Harry."

"Yes," said Melody. "I had a jewel case very like it, so I put some old jewellery of my own in it and brought it here along with the stolen one. I guessed Harry might change his mind. We don't want the crooks to get it and we don't want the police to find Harry with stolen valuables."

"It's lucky the nurse decided to lock it up, though. He would have been bound to see it wasn't the one he had before."

"I thought he might still be too dazed to notice," said Melody. "He might be angry with us when he finds out but I don't believe he'll tell anyone that we have it."

"Whoa!" Carol exclaimed. "That was really smart of you, Mel, to think all that out. It gives us time to finish our investigations – then we can tell the police *and* give them the stolen necklace."

"Another thing," said Iain. "If the crooks accuse

Harry of having the necklace, the police will only find Mel's jewellery. It's doubly clever."

Melody basked in this praise and didn't let on that she hadn't really thought it all through so carefully. She had just felt that Harry would be safer if he didn't get the necklace back and everything else naturally followed.

"Shouldn't we post the necklace to the police right away?" asked Raveena. "Then no one could say Harry ever had it."

"The thing is," said Iain, "if the police announced it had been found, the crooks would leave the area and will get away with the other stuff they've stolen."

"We need a plan," said Carol, glancing at her watch. "But we can't think of one standing in this corridor. Let's get back to the manor."

They set off, hurrying now as they felt things were beginning to move. Near the exit, Carol rushed ahead – then stopped and came back, her face flushed.

"The man who was bothering Harry earlier – he's outside and he's watching the door. He must be waiting for us!"

TWELVE

CLUES AND ALARMS

The children sidled up to the doorway. Of course, only the front two, Carol and Iain, could lean out to see what was going on in the little car park in front of the hospital. The staff at the reception desk smiled in amusement, thinking that the children were playing a game. Carol, who had the best view, whispered back to the others.

"Yup! It's him, that guy who… look we can't keep calling him *that guy*. Let's call him Snubby, since he's got a snub nose."

Raveena giggled.

"So he has! I remember. He looked a bit like Tintin with a nasty expression."

Iain squeezed his head over Carol's shoulder to look.

"Look at the car he's leaning against. It's a grey SUV – I bet it's the same one that nearly ran me over."

"He's waiting for us," said Carol. "I'm sure of it."

"He can't know we have the necklace," said Melody. "Can he?"

"No. Maybe he wants to question us to find out if Harry told us anything."

"Or threaten us," said Iain, "to stop us telling the police about him – we could only describe Baldy before."

"Look!" said Carol. "That bald man with a beard coming through the car park. He's walking towards Snubby."

"That must be the other crook, Baldy," said Melody, "He's joining up with his partner in crime."

However, the bald man walked past Snubby, ignoring him, and made for the hospital entrance. At that moment two visitors, a woman and child, walked past them and out the door. They greeted the man.

"Oh! He's not our man after all," said Iain. "I suppose there are lots of bald men with beards."

Just then they saw more visitors heading for the exit.

"Let's mix ourselves up with them," said Raj. "Then Snubby won't know what to do."

"Quick, now," said Carol, as a group of three people passed through the door.

Carol, Iain and Raveena followed close, just before a young couple came up. Melody and Raj fell in behind *them*.

Snubby was taken aback. He had taken a step forward as the door opened but stopped when he saw the other visitors leaving. He stayed unmoving as the departing visitors moved into the car park. Then, as the different groups separated to find their cars, Snubby moved slowly towards them, perhaps reluctant because of the number of witnesses around. It was strangely quiet for there were few people near the hospital.

"Let's make for—" began Carol, but Iain interrupted her.

"Shhh! He's close enough to hear us. We've no time to huddle and whisper. Raj – you, Melody and Carol make a team, I'll be with Ravee."

Raveena giggled and grabbed Iain's arm, grinning. Then Iain surprised the twins by speaking in Gaelic to Raj.

"We'll head to the corner, then split up. Take your team up Bank Street, Raj. Ravee and I will follow the main road."

"Good plan!" said Raj, in as fluent Gaelic as his friend. *"We'd better go now – everyone's getting into their cars. Let's meet at the top of Main Street. There will be plenty of people there."*

"I've an idea – whichever team isn't followed should double back and have a look at that SUV. There might be clues."

"Come on," said Iain, this time in English, "he's coming for us."

They hurried off. Snubby followed after them at a brisk pace and might have caught up with them, but he was held up. A car drove in front of him and blocked his way. Not only that, the driver got out and shouted after the children. They looked back – it was the Weasel!

"Ignore him," said Carol. She laughed. "He's done us a favour, though. He's got hold of Snubby and he's talking to him."

"Do you think they're working together?" asked Raveena.

"If he is," said Iain, "he's mucked things up. He's holding Snubby back. Come on!"

This gave the children time to get some distance ahead of him. Breaking away from the reporter, he hurried after them – then was baffled when they split up. He stood, wondering, for a few moments. Then, muttering to himself, he followed the bigger group. They walked at a quicker pace now. The snub-nosed man increased his pace too.

"He's gaining on us," said Carol, looking back. "We've still got a good lead on him, though. Maybe we should run."

"No," said Raj in a low voice. "That might spoil the plan. If we lose him too soon, he'll go back to his car and he might catch Iain and Ravee."

Carol was open-mouthed in surprise – and annoyance. So that was the plan! It was just bad luck she and Melody didn't understand Gaelic. And bad luck too that Snubby had followed *their* team instead of Iain's, so they weren't the ones to double back and do the real detective work.

Iain and Raveena were already running back. They stopped at the corner to check if the Weasel was still there, but he had gone. The first thing Iain did when they reached the car was take a photograph of its license plate.

"You keep a lookout, Ravee, in case Snubby comes back."

He knelt down and examined the car wheels while Raveena peered up the road anxiously. After several minutes, he called out,

"Ravee, have you got an envelope?"

"No, sorry."

"I'll just have to put this in my hankie. Mum will be mad at me when she sees it covered in mud but there's no helping it."

Iain used a 10p coin to scrape off mud from a tyre. Embedded in it were bits of grass and several pine needles. As he stood up, he glanced through the car windows but there was nothing but old wrappers and a beer can inside.

Raveena came round beside him to look. Then, hoping to find something herself, she circled round, examining the car. Every other moment she glanced up the road, remembering she was look out.

"That's enough," said Iain, "we'd better go now."

But Raveena gave a little squeal.

"What's this funny thing at the back of the car?"

Iain came round. "It's a tow bar. I never thought to look here. Just as well you did, Ravee. That's an important clue."

He took a quick snap. Raveena beamed but looked a little puzzled.

"What's a tow bar?"

"It's a thing you need at the back of your car if it's going to tow a caravan. It means our thieves have got a caravan somewhere. It makes sense – they can park a caravan out of the way where no one will see them."

"Oh, Iain! Snubby's coming back."

Snubby saw them almost at the same time and broke into a run. Iain grabbed Raveena's hand – there was no time to discuss things – and dragged her after him, into a nearby lane. Snubby clattered down the street and after them into the lane. There was a sharp left turn uphill and when he reached halfway the lane divided in two directions. He saw there were back entrances to several houses where the children could have gone in and got out at another point.

He swore and kicked at an old can lying on the ground. Returning, he examined his car. The little pests didn't seem to have done anything to it. He banged his fist on the bonnet. Then he got into the vehicle and drove off.

Raveena and Iain met up with the others as arranged, all of them tremendously excited. Things had taken a little longer than they had expected, so they caught their bus first and exchanged news in whispers in the back seats some distance from the other passengers. Raj was particularly excited.

"This is a breakthrough. I'm sure we can find the crooks hideout from what you've found."

"It's somewhere where there are pine trees," explained Iain. "There's a lot of pine trees in Scotland but not so many around here."

"It's a smart idea when you think of it," said Carol. "If the police are searching for someone, they'll check hotels and the like. They'd not think of a caravan."

"They might search the caravan sites around here," said Iain, "but if they just have a small caravan, they could park it on any bit of spare ground out of sight from the road."

"Hidden by trees," said Raj. "Pine trees!"

"Yes. And it wouldn't be the glen – the trees there are on hills or rough ground and there's only one narrow road. They couldn't hide a caravan because you couldn't get it in near the woods."

"They wouldn't go north because there's no cover that way if you stay near the road – which you'd have to with a caravan."

"So it has to be south – west takes you into the sea. We have an idea now where these crooks are hiding out."

"I spotted the tow bar," said Raveena, looking and sounding very smug. No one minded: they were too excited that the clues had been so useful.

"I suppose we were too worried about you being knocked off your bike to notice the tow bar when we saw the car before," said Melody. She gave out a loud yawn.

"Never mind, Mel," said Carol. "We'll soon be home and you can go straight to bed."

"We all can," said Iain, yawning too. "Though we'd better check first to see if Oswald's arranged any extra filming for us in the morning."

Carol groaned. "I'll bet he has!"

"Before that," said Raj, "I'd better get these latest clues recorded in our dossier. And before that, I'd better have something to eat."

They discovered that they did have to work the next morning.

"But we'll have the afternoon free again," said Carol as she read the schedule on the main hall wall. "We could search for the crook's hiding place then."

"There could be lots of hiding places," said Iain. "We'll have to use our bikes. The bus won't stop to let us search one place and wait to take us on to the next one."

"It's still worth trying – we might get lucky."

Raj thought of something just then and said, "I'm going to phone my aunt—"

"Not now, Raj," said his sister. "You know she likes to go to bed early."

"Well, first thing tomorrow. I hope she's in a good mood, I've got a big favour to ask."

He went off to find a snack before joining the rest of them upstairs.

Raj had finished updating the 'crime dossier' on his laptop. He had taken a photo of the pine needles and added that along with the photos of the car. The girls had gone to their bedroom and the boys were gazing out of the dormer window, lazily putting off going to bed. The sky was fairly clear so although the sun was set, the highland 'gloaming' lent a soft glow to everything. Iain yawned. Then he suddenly sat up.

"There's someone moving about out there. I can see a light."

"Why would they be using a torch?" said Raj. "It's still light enough to see by."

"Out in the open, yes," said Iain, leaning over Raj's shoulder and pressing his face to the windowpane behind him. "But it's getting dark now at the back among the bushes and trees."

Raj peered out in the same direction. A flickering light was moving about the undergrowth at the back of the manor.

"Could it be a security guard?" he asked. "The Laird said he was putting more people on patrol."

"Let's go and find out!"

Iain grabbed his torch and was almost out of the room before his friend could argue with him. Raj took a moment to find his own torch before going after him. Their clattering down the stairs alerted the girls.

"Hey! Wait for us!" Carol called out. "Wait till we get some clothes on!"

But Raj did not want to let Iain go off on his own. Who knows what danger he might be running into? He was so foolhardy sometimes! It never occurred to Raj that he could be in as much danger as Iain alone, if it *was* one of the crooks that was out there. Down they went, down the main stairs at first then the narrow backstairs which led to the servants' quarters and the warren of passages that led to the kitchen. Here they were brought to a sudden stop.

"What are you kids doing here? You should be in your beds."

It was one of the security guards, one they had not seen before.

"What are *you* doing here?" Iain did not mean to be cheeky; he was genuinely surprised.

"Not that it's any of your business but since we had a burglary the other day the police suggested we keep an eye on this back door. We only bothered to watch the front door before to keep tourists from wandering in."

"We might have known the Laird would have extra security indoors as well as in the grounds," said

Raj. He turned round at the sound of footsteps. "Oh! Hi, girls. See, they've put a guard at this door in case the burglars come back."

The girls joined them, breathing a little heavily from chasing after them.

"Are you here all day then?" asked Iain. "I mean, even when the servants are around?"

"None of your business – except that you lot had better stick to going in and out by the front entrance from now on. And stay indoors, too, when you should be in bed."

Iain groaned. "We saw a light out the back from our window. Someone's sneaking about out there."

"You said it," said Carol, rather cheekily. "Everyone ought to be indoors at this time of night."

The guard looked at them suspiciously. Iain rather admired the fact that he was not impressed by the young 'stars' and was doing his job fairly and honestly.

"We really did see something, sir," he said. "Our window looks over the rear gardens as far as the zoo fence. I don't think anybody here would be wandering about there at night."

Despite being suspicious that they might be up to some mischief, the guard decided he had better check things out. He detached a rather bulky two-way radio from his belt and spoke into it.

"Charley-X-4 to Oscar-1, reply, please."

Over some crackling came a female voice:

"This is Bobbie. What's up, Ricky?"

Ricky the guard winced at this lapse into non-official language.

"Someone in the house thinks they saw lights round the back. I'm going to investigate. Join me on the main path and we'll check it out together."

He unlocked the door and went out, pulling the door behind him.

"Stay here," he said. "In fact, go back to your beds."

He locked the door. Like a shot, Carol grabbed the spare key beside the door.

"Oh, Carol!" said Melody. "You'll get us into trouble."

However, neither she nor any of the others tried to stop her as she fumbled with the key in the lock. With a sudden click the door opened.

"Come on!"

"Look, keep quiet," said Iain. "Or that guard will be back. If we're going to follow him, we'd better do it carefully."

"Right-O!" and out Carol went, Iain following close behind.

Raj pulled them back before they'd taken more than a few steps.

"Lock the door! We'll be in real trouble if someone gets in because we left the door open."

"We'll get into trouble anyway if we chase after the guards," complained Melody. But she followed them anyway as they trotted after the guard. They kept to the grass so that their footsteps would not give them away. Ricky stopped at the end of the path and glanced at his watch. He stood for a few minutes, forcing the children to hide behind a bush in case he should turn and see them. Then there was the sound of footsteps and another guard appeared. It was Bobbie, with Sasha in tow. Luckily there was no wind to blow their scent in the dog's direction. Ricky spoke quietly to Bobbie.

"It'll be these kids imagining things, but we had better check it anyway."

They set off towards the rear of the grounds, past the stables and workshops. The children hurried after them. They felt excited as they left the partly lit area at the rear of the house and moved into the gardens and lawns further away. At first the two guards walked steadily without seeming to be much bothered about whether they came across anybody or anything. Then they suddenly stopped and pointed. The children stopped too: they grabbed each other in excitement. Up ahead, in one of the little wooded areas that bordered the manor grounds, a light was moving. Someone was creeping about, just beyond the trees.

"What on earth are they up to?" whispered Carol.

"The fence that closes in the open-air zoo runs by there," said Melody. "Don't you remember?"

Before Carol could reply, Ricky the guard shouted

and began to run. Sasha followed eagerly, pulling Bobbie along. The children ran after them, no longer bothered about being spotted: they wanted too much to see what was happening. There was a sudden shout and they saw the torch light go out. There was more shouting mixed with the sound of someone forcing their way through the undergrowth. Then they heard the voice of Ricky the guard shouting more clearly this time.

"There he goes!"

THIRTEEN

A GREAT DISCOVERY

There was a snapping sound as the intruder burst through low branches and they saw a dark shape run into the open across the grounds. Iain flicked his torch on and tried to catch the runner in its beam, but he

evaded it and disappeared into one of the gardens. Then with a crashing sound the guards burst out from the wood and ran towards them.

"Oh, Iain," groaned Melody. "What on earth made you do that? They think we're one of the burglars."

Iain switched his torch off, but it was too late. Ricky caught them in the beam of his powerful flashlight as he and Bobbie ran up. Sasha barked a friendly greeting.

"What! You little pests again!" Ricky was furious. He turned to Bobbie. "Look, I'll radio the guards at the front to come round. They might catch him before he gets out on the north side."

"Tell them he tried to cut the fence again," said Bobbie. "Luckily, it's not too bad – we stopped him before he could do much damage. I don't think anything dangerous will get out, but it will need fixing soon."

"Yeah, we stopped him just in time. You kids – get back indoors. You've caused enough trouble for tonight."

"I like that!" said Carol. "If it wasn't for us, you wouldn't have known there was someone sneaking about out here."

"And thanks to you, he got away. Now – get back inside."

They walked off towards the house, slowly and reluctantly. After a few minutes, Carol looked back, but Ricky was still there watching them.

"On your way!" he shouted.

"I suppose that's it for tonight," said Raj. "Do you think they'll catch whoever it was?"

"That lot!" Carol was still annoyed at being stopped from joining in the pursuit. "They couldn't catch a cold! Hey! That must've been the same guy that cut the fence before. I didn't get a good look at him but I'm sure he wasn't one of your friends."

"Yes," said Melody, "he seemed quite big – and sort of beefy. We couldn't see his face but I think he must have been much older than any of your friends in the WFF."

"I know he wasn't any of my friends," said Iain, "but no one will take our word for it. That's three times that's happened, now. I don't think that's ordinary vandalism. Someone is trying to get the WFF people into trouble."

And it seemed Iain was right. They had to go to bed, but next morning when they went down to breakfast, they heard that the intruder *had* escaped. The Laird was fuming and made it clear he thought the WFF were to blame and he was going to get them all arrested. The police arrived almost before they finished eating and began to interview everyone who had seen anything. This meant that the children were interviewed too. PC Cowan, who spoke to them, only seemed interested in whether they could describe the man they saw running away.

Iain emphasised that he was sure the man was nothing like any of the people he knew in the WFF. The policeman grinned at this.

"I'm sure you're right. I know some of them pretty well – used to be in it myself once."

Iain's face showed surprise and relief all at once. That was some good news at least, he thought.

"Did you find any clues?" asked Carol, who still hoped to help solve the mystery of the intruder.

PC Cowan, a young, fair-haired man, laughed.

"That is *sub judice*," he said. "It was good that you spotted something funny going on but just you leave it to us to find clues and arrest suspects. You've got plenty of work to do anyway from what I hear."

And so they had. They had barely finished the interview when they were collared and sent down to the Barn studio. Martin and Susie were there, and they were all to play in front of the blue screen and pretend they were being attacked by a dragon. Exciting as it seemed on the written page, the actual filming was rather dull. Oswald, the director, wanted them to be seen fighting the dragon from lots of different angles so they had to repeat the same actions and say the same lines over and over again. It began to get very boring especially as there wasn't actually any dragon there. A few times they had to repeat a shot because one of them was looking at the wrong place and not at the part of the non-existent dragon they were supposed to be looking at. They all did their best and if there was not much fun in this type of filming, they had a kind of satisfaction in doing their work well. They were beginning to feel a bit tired and quite hungry again when Oswald shouted,

"Cut! That's all for now, people. We'll stop for a break."

They met up with Raveena who had been watching from a chair off camera. She yawned.

"We were up so late last night I'm still tired. I'm afraid I dozed off during some of the scenes."

"I don't blame you," said Melody, "some of it has been pretty dull today."

She slurped at her cola.

"Where's Raj? Is he not interested in the film anymore?"

Raveena giggled.

"He got up early for once and phoned Aunt Nyra about something. She came in her car and picked him up. He wouldn't tell me what it was about."

"I've been looking at the script," said Iain. "We should get away before lunch time. That will give us time to have a look at the ground where we saw the fence-cutter last night."

As it happened, they were all let off a half hour later while shooting continued with the adult actors. They got changed as quickly as possible and shot off straight to the part of the grounds where they had seen the intruder the night before.

"I see they've fixed the fence," said Melody. "At least no wild animals got out."

"They haven't captured the wolf that escaped," said Raveena. "I heard some of the crew talking between takes. It was on the local radio news."

"Speaking of wolves," said Iain, "look who's coming."

They all turned sharply, then relaxed. Raveena did a little skip.

"Sasha!"

The guard dog gave a friendly bark and hurried up the slope towards them, pulling Bobbie after her. They all took turns to pat her and stroke her fur and she in return licked hands and faces and put up her odd white paw to be shaken.

"Still trying to catch our intruder?" Bobbie asked. "Don't worry, I won't tell on you. You can't do any harm now he's long gone."

"Are you investigating?" asked Carol.

"No!" Bobbie laughed. "I'm off duty just now but Sasha needs a bit of proper exercise instead of our slow walks round the perimeter."

Raveena gave Bobbie a wide-eyed look, the look of a little child hoping to get a sweet. Bobbie laughed again.

"All right, you can walk Sasha for a bit. She's tiring me out." She handed the leash to Raveena. "Keep a good grip, she's stronger than you think. I'll have a seat in the Prince's garden – bring her to me there when she's tired you out."

Raveena took the leash, but finding herself being dragged along too quickly, relinquished it to Iain. Even he had to use all his strength to keep the lively dog in check. Carol waited until Bobbie was out of sight, then said,

"Let's have a quick look round and see if we can pick up the trail of the burglar – or whatever he is."

There was nothing to be seen at the fence – the guards and the workmen who had repaired the fence had trampled all over the ground. They went into the little wooded area and soon found the trail the intruder had taken. Broken branches and crushed plants and twigs showed where he – and the guards who chased him – had gone. The trail soon became difficult to follow, but here Sasha became a great help. She had been following the trail with them, head down and sniffing, and she must have caught a scent. She pulled them off in a new direction and Iain was dragged along after her. They came to a little sheltered grove.

"Sasha's on the trail," said Carol. "And look – some clear footprints. It's muddy here and they're as clear as anything."

"Some of these are the prints of the guards," said Iain. "I suppose one of them must belong to our intruder."

"Well, let's take a photograph of all of them,"

said Melody, "and we can compare them with the other footprint."

She pulled out her mobile from its little belt pouch and took a few snaps.

"There! That should do. We'll compare the prints this evening when we get back."

"OK," said Carol. "Let's see if we can find anything else. Hurry! We'll have to go back for lunch soon."

They ran across the large, open green but they could not find any other trace of the intruder. However, as they neared the hedge which surrounded one of the gardens, Sasha dragged Iain off towards it.

"She's caught the scent again," he called back.

They went in and saw it was the Ladywell garden, where they had previously followed the burglar's trail. There were no footprints but there were some marks in the grass that might have been where someone ran through. They followed this to the little folly but there was nothing more. They sat down on the stone steps of the folly and looked round, hoping to see some other clue.

Sasha circled round and round now, almost snarling at Iain.

"You know," said Iain, "there's something funny about this but I can't quite put my finger on it."

"You mean, that we've ended up in this garden again?" said Melody.

"This place really does feel mysterious," said Raveena.

"There are different ways out," said Carol, "and the high hedge would hide which way he took. That maybe explains why he went this way."

Iain was staring at an odd mark in the folly, wondering what it was. Then Sasha leapt up and sniffed at it. This brought his attention to a little piece of wire stuck in a crack in the base just where the dog was sniffing. Looking closer, he saw it wasn't a crack. It was a thin, curved line that seemed to be carved in the stone. He leapt up with a sudden shout, causing Sasha to jump and then bark an accompaniment to him.

"What's up?" asked Carol. "Did you sit on a pin?"

"No, but there's one stuck in here. Look."

"So what? What are you doing now?"

Iain searched around the statues, pulling at bits and pieces. One of the statues held a long stone staff and he pulled and twisted this. All at once there was a click and the statue moved slightly. Iain pushed and the statue sank a little so that part of its low pedestal was sunk beneath the carved line.

"Give me a hand!"

They all got into the folly and pushed, while Sasha barked encouragement. The statue moved with a low grating noise as it crept across the stone base.

"Jumping giraffes!" exclaimed Carol. "A secret passage!"

"A man couldn't get through that gap," said Raveena, "unless he was very thin."

"A big, strong man could move the statue further than we can," said Iain, "and squeeze through. Oof! Sasha, come back!"

He pulled at the leash to drag the guard dog away from the gap.

"She must smell something," said Raveena. "Maybe the burglar."

"Maybe she thinks she'll find a giant rabbit down there," said Carol.

She leaned into the entrance, holding the statue arm so not to fall into it. She tried to use her mobile on its torch setting to see into the dark opening but it was not strong enough.

"All I can make out is mouldy old steps – I think it must go down a good way before it turns into a proper passage. Yuck! It smells old and earthy, like an old grave."

The children all looked around at each other. This was big! Should they change their plans and explore the secret passage instead? Carol opened her mouth to speak, and then stopped. She looked around.

"What's that noise? Can any of you hear it?"

None of them did at first, so they got out from the folly and listened hard.

"It sounds like someone switched on an electric fan," said Melody. "It's getting closer, I think."

Raveena jumped up, arms in the air, laughing.

"It's Raj! It's Raj! He got Aunt Nyra to take him home to collect his helicopter."

Her friends looked up, for a moment half-expecting to see a huge flying machine descending on them. They saw nothing at first, partly because they were looking for the wrong thing in the wrong place. Then they saw a blue and grey machine flying over the hedge and coming towards them. Carol laughed.

"It's a toy! But it's huge, you could fly a kitten, or even a small pup in it."

Raj's voice came from beyond the hedge.

"It's not just a toy – it's a valuable eye-spy-in-the-sky."

The helicopter dipped down and hovered in front of them at almost eye level.

"Wow!" Raj's voice came again. "Is that a secret passage in the folly?"

They looked round, searching for Raj, but all they could see was the folly and the hedge. Raveena laughed.

"There's a camera built into the helicopter and he can see us on his remote control."

"Extra-cool!" cried Carol, and she waved at the helicopter.

"No need to do that, I'm here," said Raj, bursting through a gap in the hedge and into the garden. He fiddled with the control pad he was holding and his helicopter settled on the ground. They all gathered round and peered at the controls. A miniature screen showed their ankles and feet. Raj switched it off and then, pressing another button, displayed an image.

"It's us!" said Melody. "It takes photos."

"And there's the folly behind us," said Iain. He looked up at Raj. "I never knew you had this – why didn't you tell me?"

"I only got it recently, from money I got selling stuff on eBay. I didn't say anything because I wanted to practise with it before I told anyone. There's no point showing off your helicopter if you can't fly it properly."

"This would be perfect for spying out the crooks' caravan," said Carol. "But how can you carry it when we'll have to go on bikes."

"I brought my own bike along with its trailer – I'll box the helicopter and carry it in that."

"I don't suppose you remembered to bring my bike?" Raveena frowned for the first time since they had met her. Her brother's jaw dropped and he stood, open-mouthed in embarrassment.

"Codfish!" said Raveena. "You look like a codfish!"

Melody laughed, then told Raveena.

"There are spare bikes in the manor. Susie has one and she's working today so you can borrow hers. She's so small you might not even need to lower the saddle."

"What about the secret passage we've discovered?" asked Iain. "Shall we split up into teams again?"

"Ugh!" said Melody and Raveena together.

"I'm not going down there unless all of us go," said Melody.

"Well," said Iain, slightly reluctantly. "I suppose we ought to tell someone—"

"No!" Carol spoke loudly and firmly. "Oswald and the Laird have treated us like little kids, even after we really helped out, like with the wolves. I vote we wait until we've found out as much as we can about it before we tell anyone."

"All right," said Melody, "but only for a day or two. We've got to think about poor Harry. If we find something that will help him, we've got to let him know as soon as possible."

"Of course," said Carol. "Let's get this entrance closed. We'll explore the passage later – maybe this evening if things go well."

FOURTEEN

THE SEARCHERS

They couldn't start right away of course. They were going by way of Ardriagh, which would take an hour to reach on bike. So they packed food and drink into backpacks and made sure their bikes were all in good working order. Melody was the last to join the little group.

"I found this little map," she said. "It's basic but it will give us some idea of where things are."

They all gathered round as she showed them the map.

"We can ignore the camp site," said Iain, pointing to a spot just south of Ardriagh. "There's too many folk around there."

"Yes," said Raj. "But they'll still need some kind of road, even if it's a bit rough and ready."

Iain found a bit of a pencil in his pocket and marked lines on Melody's map.

"These are the roads I remember. See, they go inland – that's where you'll get pine trees. These woods are called *Coilltean Samhach*. You know, it's funny but one of these roads goes towards *An Sloc Beag*."

"That's where the houses belonging to rich folk are, isn't it?" said Carol. "They may have burgled one of them."

"They've got a nerve if that's true," said Raj. "Imagine hiding out so close to a place you've just robbed."

"Don't forget what Harry told us," said Melody. "Some local crook told them when the owners would be away on holiday. Folk could be robbed and not know it yet."

"Well, that gives us a plan," said Carol. "We'll check out these two side roads first. Everybody ready?"

They were. So they set off.

For a while, they almost forgot they were on a quest. The sun warmed them and a light sea-breeze ruffled their hair and T-shirts. It was a glorious afternoon. A bus passed them and half a dozen cars, going both ways, but otherwise they saw no traffic.

"I wonder why it's so quiet," Iain called back to the others. They discovered the answer when they reached Ardriagh and stopped for a brief rest.

"Look!" cried Carol.

A large poster was pasted on a noticeboard. It showed a picture of a wolf's head and in large print proclaimed *Wolf at Large!* Beside it was another poster which made the others laugh. It was a picture of Carol and Melody, one of several posters about town advertising the movie they were filming. Only someone had drawn wolf's ears and whiskers on their faces.

"I don't think that's funny!" Carol said, scowling.

Melody merely shook her head and smiled. A woman, holding the hand of a girl of about seven, came up to them.

"Never you mind about these daft gowks," she told Carol. "They haven't the sense God gave geese. Some fools like to blame outsiders for everything."

"And we're outsiders?" said Carol.

"Aye – well not all of you. I recognise you two – *Rash* and *Rafie*, isn't it? – I used to see you with your dad. He's my GP."

Raj and Raveena forbore to correct her pronunciation of their names. To their surprise, she asked for autographs.

"My wee lassie loved you in that series, *The Slight Princess*."

"*Light Princess*," Melody corrected. That had been

a TV series where they had both shared the same part. Though, as Carol said later,

"I hate having to play these soppy parts. They're fine for Melody but I prefer parts where you do things, not float about in the air."

Melody punched her sister at this and the usual tussle between them ensued – but that was later. Now, they smiled and signed happily. In fact, they all signed – Raveena with a giggle at the idea of being asked for an autograph. Several passers-by, noticing this, came over and also asked for autographs. Fortunately not too many did, as they wanted to get on quickly.

"We'll have to get you into a scene in the film," Melody told the Akashs, "to justify that poor woman asking for your autographs."

"Oh, yes! Can you?" Raveena did a little jump.

Raj said nothing as his mouth was full of the sandwich he'd taken from his pack. He had to swallow it quickly as they got ready to cycle on.

"These wolf posters are up everywhere," said Melody as they made their way through the town traffic.

"What do you expect?" said Iain, who was just behind her. "Hey, Carol! Take the next left – it's a lot quicker."

Ignoring loudly sounded horns, they got off Main Street and soon got through the town. After they were about ten minutes or so into the countryside, Raj shouted out from the back,

"When are we going to stop to eat!"

They had a quick snack and then Iain took the lead again, since he knew the area best – apart from Raj who preferred to stay in the rear so no one would run into his trailer and upset his precious cargo. They soon passed the caravan site which looked busy and bustling. There were plenty of trees, but they were well spaced out so it obviously would not have been a good place to hide even if it had not been so busy. They cycled along at a leisurely pace, for the road was flat and there was only the lightest of breezes blowing against them. Through the trees they caught glimpses of distant yachts dipping and turning on the waves. At least four of them did. Iain kept his eyes on the other side of the road, looking out for the turnings leading inland. A gap came up, half hidden by bush and undergrowth: he shouted back,

"That's not it! The next one's what we want!"

The others looked up sharply as they whizzed by. They hadn't even noticed it. They gazed with more attention now at the woods to their left, thick with several kinds of trees, including Scots pines. They travelled another kilometre and a half however before they saw the turning they were searching for. They pulled up and gathered round, just off the main road.

"It's pretty narrow," said Raj, "and pretty rough too. Could they get a caravan up there?"

Carol peered into the gloom created by the thick, overhanging branches of the trees.

"I think they could, provided it doesn't get any narrower further in. It doesn't look like it's much used."

They pushed their bikes on a little further until they came to a broader, open area where the way divided and went in three directions.

"Which way do we go now?" asked Melody.

Raj laughed. "We don't go anywhere, at least not yet." He bent over and began to unstrap the box that held his helicopter. "It's got a range of about 150 metres – it can fly far further but I'd start to lose control of it. The control signal wouldn't reach it."

"Oh," said Carol, disappointed for a moment. Then, brightening, "We can check an area, then bring it back and move on to another area."

"That will take ages," said Melody. "We'll have to be dead lucky."

"We'll need some luck," said Raj, standing up with the helicopter in his arms. "But it's not as bad as you think. We can walk with the control pad, so we can go further. It won't be very fast but we don't need to bring it back every few minutes. I'll need to change the batteries every half hour or so, though."

"We don't want to be pushing our bikes through the wood," said Iain. "Let's hide them behind those bushes over there."

They hid their bikes and the trailer while Raj got his helicopter set up. Iain carried the spare batteries, and they were all ready to go. They felt like they were about to set off but they didn't, not at first.

"We'd take all day exploring this wood," said Raj. "What I'm going to do first is send the helicopter up as far as it can safely go. That will let us see a large area all at once."

"Good idea!" said Iain. "They can't have hidden their caravan under a tree – it would need a bit of space. You should be able to see some gaps in the wood where it might be parked."

Raj switched on the power and the helicopter blades began to spin, the fan-like sound became louder. They all gave a cheer as it took off, straight up towards the sky. Then they gathered round Raj, crushing against each other to get a look at the little screen on the control panel. At first, all they saw was the green, leafy roof of the wood, divided by the three lanes that ran through it.

"Look! There's us!" Raveena squealed and looked upwards, waving.

"Don't be so daft," said her brother, but half-heartedly, for he had to concentrate on the helicopter. "I'll make it do a fifty-metre circle and see if that shows up anything."

He moved the control and the helicopter swung eastwards for about fifty metres, then circled round until it disappeared, hidden by the treetops.

"Can you control it behind all these trees?" asked Melody.

"Sure! It uses a radio signal, not an infrared beam like some toy helicopters. This is a serious machine." He said the last with a note of pride.

"Look," said Carol, "that northern track gets narrower as it goes along – I'm sure they couldn't get the caravan up there."

Raj directed the helicopter southwards, still circling. They saw the green roof again and for a moment it seemed like an endless emerald carpet below them.

"There's the south track," said Iain, but the helicopter continued to circle.

"We don't know if these lanes, tracks or whatever won't turn back on themselves," said Raj. "I'll keep it circling and if we don't see anything, we'll have to pick one path and follow it."

The first reconnaissance showed nothing, except that the two remaining lanes did not get narrower like the first. Carol tossed a coin and they started walking south rather than east. Raj kept the helicopter hovering above them until they had walked about a hundred metres and sent it round again on another circle, further southwards. A couple of open areas showed up this time but there was no sign of any kind of vehicle, or any lane leading into the gaps. They walked on, still hopeful, though with a growing worry that they might have chosen the wrong path. About twenty minutes and half a kilometre later, they had found nothing worth investigating. Raj brought the helicopter back down and replaced the batteries.

"Let's try one more sweep further on," said Carol, "then go back and try the other lane."

To save power, Iain and Carol carried the helicopter between them for a hundred metres or so, then it was sent to fly up above the wood again. Now they began to see more gaps, though at first no sign of a car or caravan. One gap showed a pool, another a brook running through it; another showed open grass but no vehicles. As the helicopter flew past this last gap, two birds flew up straight at the machine. Raj frantically twisted his controls to make his helicopter swerve out of the way.

"Whew! That was close – if one of these birds had hit the blades it would have crashed."

"It wouldn't have done the bird much good either," said Raveena. "The poor thing."

"My poor helicopter! Wait a minute – look!"

The helicopter, veering off wildly to avoid the birds, had pointed its camera at an angle looking across the trees rather than down on them. There was too much angle to see down to the ground, but there was a clear gap between the tops of the trees – and smoke. Thin wisps of smoke which faded soon after they came above the treetops, but smoke all the same.

"You don't get smoke without—" began Carol.

"Fire?" said Raveena, with a giggle.

"A fire means people," said Iain. "Maybe a camp site."

"Don't they have a caravan?" said Melody. "It would have something to heat things up."

"It still could be worth checking out," said Carol.

Raj was already guiding the aircraft towards the smoke to investigate. They all crowded close to Raj once more, peering at the screen. They saw the gap in the trees as the helicopter approached the smoky column, then it soared over the open area. As it swooped round, they saw two men standing over a fire. They seemed to be breaking up boxes and tearing rags to throw on the fire. They were too engrossed with what they were doing to notice the sound of the miniature helicopter high above them.

"What are they doing?" asked Melody, quite puzzled.

"That's stuff they probably carried their swag in," said Raj, using a phrase from an old-fashioned detective novel. "Their fingerprints and DNA will be all over it."

The helicopter circled round now and they saw the caravan, and alongside it the grey SUV.

"Get a snap of that, quick," said Carol.

Raj's finger pressed the button one, two, three times quickly: each time the screen froze for a moment, showing a photograph had been taken. Then the helicopter swerved past and round again to hover behind the smoke. One of the men looked round then up, but he didn't spot the machine and turned back to his work.

"That looked like Snubby," said Iain. "He's wearing the same clothes from when we saw him the other day."

"The other man must be Baldy," said Carol. "But he's wearing a hoodie."

Raj brought the helicopter round again, moving it towards the men, taking a snapshot as it went downwards.

"Careful, Raj!" said Iain. "They're bound to spot it if you go any lower. They'll hear it coming."

Raj made the helicopter swerve and climb. As it circled back its camera caught one man looking upwards; Snubby was pointing at it and shaking his partner's arm. The other shook him off and shrugged. He was bent back over their fire when the children lost sight of the men. Raj had brought his little aircraft back over the trees and out of sight.

"Bring it back," said Iain, "and we can check that the photos have all been saved. We don't need to take any more risks than we need to."

"What risks?" said Carol, a little scornfully. "They can't get at the helicopter and they can't tell where we are, so we're perfectly safe."

"If they got a good look at the helicopter, they might see it has a camera. That's why I didn't want Raj to let it get too near them."

"I guessed that too," said Raj. "That's why I

brought it up quickly. If they knew they were being spied on, they'd be bound to make a run for it and they'd never be caught."

"At least, not by us," said Raveena. "They'd be caught in London or somewhere and we'd never get any credit."

"We're supposed to be doing this to help Harry," said Melody, "not to show how clever we are."

"Of course," Raveena beamed a broad smile. "But we can have fun as well – and get credit too."

The helicopter landed beside them. Raj brought out his mobile and connected it to the control pad. In a few minutes he had loaded the pictures onto his phone. He swiped through the images and they all looked on, relieved to see clear pictures of the car, the caravan and the two men. Raj swiped with his fingers to zoom in. One figure's face was clear.

"It *is* Snubby!"

"We've got real evidence now," said Iain. "We ought to get back."

"Yes," said Raj. "Let's hope the crooks thought it was just a flying toy someone was playing with. If they don't realise it was spying on them, everything will be fine."

Iain had to smile at Raj's *just a flying toy.* His helicopter *was* a flying toy – even if it was a very sophisticated and extremely clever toy. But it had done the job brilliantly. They had almost everything they needed now.

"Shall we help carry the helicopter again?" Carol said to Raj who was on his knee beside it, checking everything was in good order. Everyone was gathered round admiring the gleaming, blue machine. Then from behind them came a low, threatening, growling sound. They turned and everyone gasped with horror at what they saw: it was the escaped wolf!

FIFTEEN

CRYING WOLF

For a moment a silly thought went through Iain's head: *the wolf doesn't look anything like its picture on the posters.* It seemed bigger, somehow, than he remembered. Of course, the last time they had been at the top of a tower, looking down. Now, the wolf was a mere five or six metres away from them, glowering and growling at them.

"I d-don't like the w-way it's looking at us," said Raj. "It looks as if it's trying to d-decide which one of us to eat first."

Iain could hear the fear in his friend's voice. Carol was breathing in sharp gasps, Melody and Raveena were hugging each other tightly. Iain himself felt like it was winter, with cold wrapping his body, and that he would start shivering any moment. But a part of his mind was still calm, though the rest of him was thoroughly scared. All of them were afraid. Really, really frightened. The calm part of Iain's mind noticed the blood on its mouth – and on its teeth when it snarled. At the side of the lane lay a dead rabbit, which it had dropped when it saw them. It now began to move slowly towards them. Did it think one of them would make a much better meal than a rabbit? They all stood, frozen. Their instinct was to run, but they knew that it would chase after them. *Running things were to be run down and killed – and eaten!* That was how a wolf would think. Iain put a hand out and felt Raj's shoulder. He managed with great difficulty to keep his voice calm and said, in a hoarse whisper,

"Raj, get up slowly… keep the control pad ready to use."

Raj was puzzled and confused. However, he did as he asked. As he rose, the wolf snarled again and began to move more quickly towards them, its head down as if preparing to attack. Now, Raj realised what Iain's idea was. He pressed buttons quickly. The helicopter blades spun, humming, making the wolf slow down and prick up its ears in puzzlement. The machine took off, rising above the children's heads. The wolf stopped and cocked its head, for the first time a little bit wary. Then Raj sent the helicopter flying towards it, level with its head. The wolf scampered back several metres but snapped at the machine as it swerved close to it. It growled, but this time it was an uncertain, defensive growl. The helicopter circled and the wolf turned with it, now much less sure of itself. It had never seen anything like this before – it was larger than most birds but it flew more like an insect than a bird. Perhaps it was some kind of giant wasp.

"Well done, Raj!" cried Carol. "You've got it on the run."

"Quiet!" hissed Iain. "You'll draw its attention back to us." In a whisper he said, "Keep it up Raj, you're doing great."

The wolf momentarily stopped and glared back at the children, but Raj brought the helicopter back in front of it, distracting it once more. He made it move up and down in front of the animal, move away then rush at its nose, veering off at the last moment. In this way, the wolf was made to move back, slowly but surely. Carol had an inspiration. Moving slowly so not to catch the wolf's attention, she edged forward a few metres. Then, in one quick movement she lifted the dead rabbit, and flung it towards the wolf. The wolf looked at the helicopter, then at the rabbit, indecisive for a moment. Then it snapped up the dead animal and trotted off. A rabbit in the mouth was much better than a giant insect in the wood. They all held their breaths for several long seconds, then as the wolf disappeared into the trees, everyone let out a sigh of relief.

"That poor rabbit," said Raveena, almost in tears. "How could you throw it to the wolf!"

"It was already dead," said Carol, "and the wolf might have come back if we hadn't let it have it."

Melody cuddled the younger girl.

"It's just shock," she said. "She'll be fine in a moment. I think we'd better go home now."

"Yes," said Carol. "We've done everything we planned – and a bit more. Imagine running into that wolf here. It's miles away from where we last saw it."

Iain pointed to the east. "Over the hills you see above the trees is the glen where we saw the wolf pack. It must have wandered from there and maybe liked the wood here."

Raj replaced his helicopter's batteries once more and while Iain and Carol carried it he held his control pad close, peering about for any sign of the wolf's return. However they got safely back to the junction where they had hidden their bikes and were soon heading out of the wood. Iain stopped them when they came to the main road. He left his bike and from the cover of a bush, looked up and down the road. A moment later he came running back.

"Hide!" he told them and grabbed his bike, dragging it into the woody area. The others couldn't think what had excited him, but a moment later they saw a grey SUV heading northward to Ardriagh. It was out of sight in a few seconds but they could just make out the driver.

"Snubby!" Carol was ecstatic. "That's great! It means they didn't guess they were being spied on. They won't make a run for it and we can still see them arrested up here – on our evidence."

After all the excitement, the trip back seemed dull, tedious and tiring. When they reached Ardriagh, Raj declared,

"I'm starving! And I'm tired. Let's stop for a rest and get something to eat."

This time everyone felt the same. The fresh air, the exercise and their scare had left them all…

"As hungry as wolves!" said Carol. The others didn't think this was particularly funny but they all agreed that a snack would go down well. They still had an hour's cycling to do and didn't think they could last without refuelling. Melody had another thought however.

"If we're stopping here, I'll drop into the hospital for five minutes and see how Harry's getting on."

"And see if he's discovered the trick you played on him?" said Carol, a little unkindly. Her sister's face fell. "Sorry, Mel. You did the right thing, and we'll soon be able to get the burglars arrested without Harry getting involved."

Raveena decided to accompany Melody so they separated, the others promising to buy them some food. They had stopped near the hospital, so the girls chained their bikes and were soon walking in at the front door. Melody glanced round nervously before they went in but there was no sign of a grey SUV or Snubby hanging around. The visit was to be something of let down – but also something of a surprise. They met a nurse at the door of the ward.

"I'm afraid you can't speak to Mr Puddock just now. He's suffering from concussion and we've had to sedate him."

"Oh no!" said Melody. "What happened? He seemed to be getting better yesterday."

The nurse gave her a sympathetic smile.

"Concussion can affect people a day or two after the original injury. He'll be all right if he gets some rest."

Just then they heard a familiar voice from inside the ward.

"Come in, kids! It's OK to sit with Harry for a few minutes as long as you don't disturb him."

"Ronnie" cried Melody, loudly enough to get a

glare from the nurse. In a quieter voice she asked, "What are you doing here?"

Ronnie signalled the girls to pull chairs over. She glanced questioningly at Raveena and Melody explained about Iain's friends.

"They're staying with us at the manor. Why are you here? I thought you were ill."

"It was just a bad headache. I'm fine now. Thing is, I'd been complaining to everyone about Harry not fixing my necklace. Then it turned out he *had* done it and left it in my mail box at the manor. I'd missed it because I was busy and hadn't checked."

"You must have felt embarrassed."

"Yes, and I thought I ought to come and apologise. Only I can't, because he's unconscious. I hope he gets better soon."

"Is that the necklace you're wearing now?" asked Raveena.

"Yes." Ronnie undid a button of her blouse, to show it better. "You know what Harry did? He made a copy of my necklace – a cheap and cheerful one but rather nice – and left me a note, saying *next time you're doing acrobatics, wear this instead so you won't damage the real thing.* Wasn't that sweet of him?"

Ronnie opened a large handbag and took out a case which she opened, displaying the copy. It looked very nice, though the jewels were pallid compared to the real ones Ronnie was wearing.

"Well," said Ronnie, getting up, "I don't think

179

we're doing Harry much good hanging about here. Can I offer you two a lift back?"

"No thanks," said Melody. "We came by bike with the boys. They're off getting chips but I thought I'd have a quick look to see how Harry was first."

She looked at the unconscious man with some concern as she said this.

"The doctor said he'll be fine, so don't worry. It's good of you to visit."

They left Ronnie at the car park and went to their bikes. As they removed the chains, Raveena said,

"I hope the boys haven't eaten all the chips."

They hadn't; in fact they had kept some food for them, in a polystyrene box to keep it warm. On their way up, they saw them coming down and met up close to the police station.

"We got a fish supper you can share," said Carol, through a mouthful of pie. "Help yourselves."

While they ate, Raveena asked if they were going to report their sighting of the wolf now. Carol looked a bit downcast.

"Iain insisted we had to report it right away," she said, in a tone that suggested she didn't agree. "We were waiting for you, so you wouldn't be left out."

"Of course we have to eat first," said Raj, dipping a chip into tomato sauce.

"Why the long face?" Melody asked Carol.

"I just realised – if a search party goes looking for the wolf in that wood, they might frighten the crooks off before *we* can tell the police about them."

"Still, we'd better tell them – the wolf is too dangerous not to. We could tell the police about the crooks' hideout at the same time, then they can be arrested before the wolf hunt."

"It's a bit disappointing," said Raj. "We wanted to present all our evidence properly but half of it is still up at the manor on my laptop."

"Well, I don't think the burglary at the manor had anything to do with these jewel thieves," said Iain, "so there's still that mystery to solve."

While they made their way to the police station, Melody told them of Harry's relapse and the meeting with Ronnie.

"They said he'll be all right," she told the boys, seeing their worried expressions. "Here's the station now and look who's coming out – the policeman who interviewed us at the manor."

They ran towards him, pushing their bikes along with them. The constable watched their approach with an amused expression.

"What's all this now? Another burglary?"

A medley of voices shouted *wolf!* Then Carol said,

"We were down in the woods at…" she turned to Iain.

"*Coilltean Samhach.* We were cycling in the wood there when we saw it."

"Are you sure it was the wolf and not someone's lost dog?"

The children were outraged. Raj brought out his mobile and flicked through the photos he'd taken from the helicopter. Then he presented a picture to the constable. He had kept his head well enough to take a snap of the wolf when it was advancing on them.

The policeman's expression became serious.

"You children shouldn't be out on your own with that beastie on the prowl. When did you see this? Are you just back from the woods? Wait. Add the time for you buying that food to your journey back – that will be well over an hour."

"Why does it matter how long?" asked Raveena. The policeman smiled now.

"We had another report about the wolf ten minutes ago. It was seen heading away from the wood and into the hills towards the glen. I was worried for a moment that it might have doubled back. People sometimes camp out in that wood. Still, you were right to report this – thanks."

"What about the burglars?" asked Carol, as the policeman seemed to be about to leave them. "You're still looking for them, aren't you?"

"We have no leads yet on the break-in at the manor."

"What about the other break-ins, where valuable things have been stolen?" asked Melody.

The policeman lowered over them, arms akimbo, glaring at them as if they were suspects in a case.

"Now look! You children have just been very helpful. Don't spoil it by making up crimes that haven't happened. The break-in at your manor is the only big burglary that's happened recently. The only other big problem we have is that villain who is setting wild animals free to terrorise the countryside."

"But—" began Carol. Iain interrupted her.

"We're sorry, Constable. It's just that we couldn't imagine our burglary was a one-off. We thought there must be more."

"I suppose that's understandable; still other people's problems are not your business. So don't bother me again unless you have some real information."

The other children had been puzzled by Iain's insistence on letting things drop but they went along with it. This was partly because deep down they hadn't wanted to give up their investigation so soon. As soon as the policeman had gone, they demanded to know why he had stopped them telling about the burglaries.

"Don't you see? If the wolf has gone back to the glen, then they won't search the woods and frighten the burglars off. There's another thing. The police can't know about the stolen necklace or any other burglaries. Nobody knows they've been burgled yet."

"But *we* know…" said Carol. "Oh…" She slapped the top of her head. "I'm a goose! The police would wonder how *we* knew and that could give Harry away."

"We don't want to do that if we can possibly avoid it," said Melody.

"We need to have a council of war," said Raj, "to decide what we should do."

"Better do it back at the manor," said Carol, who noticed some passers-by looking at the children with interest. Normally she enjoyed attention, but they'd had an eventful, exhilarating but arduous day. She wanted to get back as soon as possible. The others felt the same and they were soon on the road to the manor.

A dog barked at them as they pedalled rather wearily through the main gate. They stopped and dismounted, expecting to see Sasha, but it was another dog, with another guard attached by the leash.

"Where's Sasha?" asked Raveena.

"Having a rest," said the guard (who they later found out was called Connor). "Even dogs need a break. This is *Gato* – he shares guard duty with Sasha and another couple of dogs. That way we always have at least one dog on patrol."

"Wait a minute," said Melody. "Doesn't *gato* mean *cat* in Spanish?"

"Yes," said Connor, laughing. "Whoever named him had a strange sense of humour."

"I thought it was *gateaux*," said Raj. "You know, French for *cake*."

They all laughed at this, for although he was friendly enough with them, Gato was a fierce-looking dog. Nobody would call him *a cake* or *a cat* to his face.

"Trust you to think of food!" said Carol.

"Huh! He's no worse than you are," said Melody. "He might talk about it more but you gobble up as much as Raj – probably more."

The barb was like water off a duck's back to Carol.

"Well, let's see if we're not too late for dinner. I'm ready for a good gobble."

SIXTEEN

UNDERGROUND LABYRINTH

They were late, but not too late to get some food. Plates of chicken legs, eggs, tomatoes and croquettes were devoured, followed by a more relaxed sweet of jelly and fruit. By the time they had finished their meal, all the other diners had left, so they decided to have their council of war there and then. Raj leaned forward, elbows on the table and his hands pressed together beneath his chin. *Just like Sherlock Holmes*, thought Iain. *Raj is being the great detective.*

"I've been thinking," said Raj. "If *we* can't tell the police about the jewel thieves because it might get Harry into trouble, we could let the police know anonymously. They often get anonymous information about crimes."

"We could send the necklace anonymously, too," said Melody.

"Yes, that would prove that jewels have been stolen," said Iain. "Though of course we can't say where they've been stolen from."

"I don't think we should send the necklace," said Carol. "What if it gets lost in the post or stolen? It's worth a fortune. Better just send a photograph."

"Good idea," said Iain. "We could add a note saying it's stolen goods."

"Yes!" Raj slammed his palms on the table. "Rich people record their valuables – with photographs – in case they're stolen."

"Of course," said Melody. "Insurance companies insist on it, for really valuable items. Our mum—"

"Our mum had to get all her best jewellery photographed," said Carol. "What *donkeys* we are, Mel. We should have thought of that right away. The police can check these records and find out who's been burgled."

"Then the police can use our evidence to arrest the burglars," said Iain. "They won't have the necklace, but I bet they've other stolen loot in their caravan."

"Look," said Raj, "I'll make sure our crime dossier is up to date – I'll add our helicopter photos and a photo of the necklace. Then I'll get it all printed out."

"Be careful no one sees what you are printing," said Iain. "Do it when no one's around."

"Tomorrow," said Carol. "We'll explore the secret passage – maybe we'll find something there that we should add to our dossier."

"We'd better not take too long sending it, or the burglars might leave the area."

"Explore in the morning, send the dossier afterwards – all done tomorrow. We'll have to post it from town so it can't be traced back to us."

"It will cost a fortune in stamps," said Raj, "but we can share that between us."

They got up now and headed off but they were intercepted in the hall by Ronnie Mere, who was carrying scripts.

"Oswald's rearranged things since I'm back at work. Tomorrow morning, first thing in the Barn studio, we're doing the scenes we should have done a couple of days ago. It's where we meet the Lord of the Light Elves."

"What's a Light Elf?" asked Raveena.

"Something to do with Norse mythology – there were light and dark elves. No one knows for sure what the difference was. For our story, Oswald has decided they were once the same people but separated long ago. The Dark Elves – Iain's playing one of these – went to live underground and became pale from living in dark caves. The Light Elves, on the other hand, stayed above ground under the sun and are brown. Ravi plays the Lord of the Light Elves – he hopes you won't bring along any wild animals, by the way."

"Ravi?" For a moment, Raveena thought Ronnie was referring to her, then she squealed. "Oh! Ravi Ansari! He's my favourite actor. Can I come and watch again. I'd *love* to meet *him*."

Ronnie smiled and peered at her thoughtfully.

"You know, you *are* a pretty girl. We could make you up as a little princess in the Light Elves' court. Would you like that? Would you like to be in the movie – just a *tiny* part, mind you?"

Raveena shrieked and flung herself into Ronnie's arms.

"I'd love it, I'd love it, I'd love it!"

"Well, make sure you report early tomorrow at the Barn," Ronnie said, trying to detach Raveena from her. "And get a good night's sleep, you lot. We'll be working you hard tomorrow. I'll have a word with Rosie about a costume for you, Raveena… now, let me go!"

So they would have to do their exploring a little later. They were a bit worried about the delay but they thought there was no helping it. The last hour or so before bedtime, the children worked at their various tasks. Raj updated their dossier. He discovered a spare printer in the little office given over to the film crew. No one was around, so he sneaked it upstairs, attached it to his laptop and printed out the dossier. He put this into a large manilla envelope he had found and hid it under Iain's mattress. Iain, Melody and Carol went off to read through their scripts.

"It's not too bad," said Carol. "Ravi and Ronnie – that sounds funny when you say it out loud – do most of the talking, so all we have to remember is where to stand, really."

Raveena spent most of the time preening herself in front of the mirror, wondering if she would get to give her favourite actor a hug. Eventually, eyes began to close, heads began to droop and beds and warm blankets beckoned.

"CUT! That's a wrap, people." Oswald's voice rang out and the cast in front of the camera gave a sigh of relief and relaxed. It had been a tiring morning but they had got a lot done. Raveena was ecstatic. Ronnie had got Oswald to agree that she could appear in the background with a few extras. However, on seeing her pretty face and bubbly personality, he decided to make her an attendant to the Elf Lord. This meant she was out in front with the star actors and even got to hold Ravi's hand at one point. She couldn't wait for the film to be shown, so all her friends could see her in it. The other children had only one thing in mind however – lunch!

Raj had had a bit of exercise while they were being filmed.

"I recharged the batteries and took my helicopter for a run – I mean, flight. I used it to check a section of the zoo fence in case it had been cut again."

"And was it?" asked Carol between mouthfuls.

"No, but I ran in into Bobbie and Ricky – and Sasha. She was curious about the helicopter but she wasn't afraid of it."

"I expect that's because you didn't fly it straight at her."

"I suppose that's it. Ricky said he wishes the guards had a few machines like it as it would save them a lot of work. Bobbie disagreed – she thought if they used helicopters or drones there'd be less work for the guards and some of them would lose their jobs."

"They couldn't replace Sasha with a helicopter," said Raveena, and they all agreed.

"She tried to chase it," Raj laughed, "and pulled her leash out of Bobbie's hand. She's still a young dog and gets over enthusiastic at times. Not like Gato. Mmm! Pass me a slice of that cake, Mel."

"Don't eat too much," said Iain. "We have to check out the secret passage."

Raj nodded his head and waved a hand (his mouth was too full of cake to speak).

"We'd better change into old clothes," said Melody. "I'm sure the passage will be filthy."

"Here it is," said Carol, slapping one of the folly pillars. "Did anyone see us come in?"

"No," said Iain. "The guards are more concerned with the zoo fence than what's happening in the gardens."

They were all dressed in old jeans and T-shirts, except Raveena, who was wearing shorts and a rather tatty anorak. The hood was up, covering her head.

"I don't want any horrible spiders or beetles falling into my hair," she told them.

They had four torches between them and Raveena had brought a large ball of string. She had remembered the old story of Theseus and the Minotaur.

The other children weren't sure it would be very useful but they said nothing, rather than disappoint her.

Melody pulled and twisted the disguised lever that unlocked the secret entrance while the others shoved like anything. With a sharp, scraping sound it moved and a narrow opening was revealed. They managed to open it wider this time, so that Carol was able to walk into the entrance without crouching or squeezing her way through. Torchlight revealed a narrow flight of ancient and very worn steps leading down into darkness. Carol could feel the cold dank air seeping up from the depths, even though she had only taken a couple of steps in from the warm garden.

"Well, don't just stand there," said Raj. "Let's go into the *deep, dark dungeon*."

"You've been playing too many *Dragons and Danger* games," said Iain.

Carol took a quick, deep breath then stepped forward, descending the narrow stairway. The others followed close behind, stepping carefully for the steps were uneven and slippery with moss. At last they reached the bottom where their flashing torches showed them a space about the size of a large room. They had an advantage being children, for the ceiling was very low – an adult would have to keep their head lowered. Three passages led off in different directions, all narrow and again easier for children to navigate than adults.

"These two go north-west and north-east," said Iain. "You know, I think they must take you to the edge of the grounds. There could easily be exits hidden there."

"That one could come out near the zoo fence," said Carol. "This could be how the fence-cutter gets in and out without being seen."

"We saw him the other night," said Melody. "But he didn't use any exit near the fence."

"The guards saw him there, thanks to us," said Iain. "He ran down here because the hedge stopped anyone from seeing him going into the secret passage."

"This other passage must go into the manor," said Raveena.

They all turned to look. The passage was narrower than the others, but the stonework was smoother and it appeared to go in a straight line unlike the other passages.

"Surely the Laird knows about the secret passages?" said Melody.

"He might not," said Iain. "They're really old and might be forgotten. It could be someone found out about them by accident."

"Now what?" said Melody. "Shall we tell someone that we've found these passages?"

"We haven't found everything yet," said Carol. "We don't know for sure that these passages go where we think they go."

They all agreed with this, for surely you couldn't find a secret passage and not explore it? Carol shone her torch all round and peered into the different tunnels.

"We don't have all day to explore. We'll be quicker if we split into two groups. One group will follow the passage that seems to lead into the manor, the other group will follow the one that goes towards the zoo fence. We can meet back here when we've found out where each passage goes."

"The passage into the house is likely to be a bit of a maze," said Iain. "Whoever follows the outside passage will probably get back quicker, and they might have quite a wait for the others."

Raveena gave a little jump and a squeal of delight.

She raised her ball of string.

"I knew this would be useful. I'll tie one end to something and let it out as we go along. Then they don't have to wait. They just have to follow the string."

Raj wanted to explore the outer passage, Melody and Raveena the inner one. Iain and Carol tossed a coin to see who joined Raj – and Carol won.

She and Raj went along the tunnel they thought led towards the zoo fence. There was a damp, earthy smell that was almost but not quite unpleasant. The walls were made of packed earth, with the odd rock protruding here and there. Every ten metres or so narrow ancient wooden beams, embedded in the walls, supported the low roof. They felt like they were deep, deep underground, though in fact the passage was gradually rising.

"We *are* going up," said Raj. "Look, you can see how it slopes now."

"Of course, the grounds slope upwards as you go away from the manor. Is it just me, or is this tunnel getting smaller?"

The tunnel *was* getting narrower and the roof lower. They could still stand up straight, but they had to move closer together and the roof was almost brushing the tops of their heads.

"An adult would have to really scrunch down to get through here," said Carol. "I suppose in olden times this was only used in a dire emergency. All that mattered would be getting away, even if you had to wriggle your way out."

They ploughed on, beginning to feel cold and damp and a little bored. They almost wished they had gone with the others into the manor. There was nothing here but the same dank walls and roof going on and on. Then, Raj stopped suddenly.

"Can you feel that? I think there's fresh air coming in. I'm sure I can smell fresh cut grass."

They hurried forward and soon they saw what looked like the end of the tunnel.

"It's a bit of an old door," said Carol. "Shove it to one side."

The door did not cover the whole of the exit. Up close, they could see that bushes hid both the door and the space it didn't cover. The door was awkward but they only had to move it a little to be able to squeeze past. Stems and leaves snatched at their faces as they squeezed out into what was blinding light after the dark tunnel. Loud barks surprised them and they turned to see a dog sprinting towards them.

"Sasha!" They both cried out as one. The guard dog leapt up at each one in turn, trying to lick their faces.

"Ugh! Get off you great beast," said Carol. "Where's your mistress?"

"There she is – she must have let her off her leash."

Bobbie came running up, panting a little. She

was out of uniform, wearing jogging trousers and a sweater. The children looked anxiously behind them but were relieved to see that the bushes completely hid the entrance.

"Hi kids! What's this?" She looked, puzzled, at their torches. "Are you playing some kind of game?"

"Yes," said Raj, suddenly inspired. "We were going to practise signalling in morse code."

Raj pressed a button on the side of his torch and it began to make short and long flashes. Carol was surprised to see that the beam was bright enough to be seen in daylight. Raj's torch really was made for signalling and he really was flashing morse code. Bobbie laughed and shook her head.

"Does your boss know you're playing with Sasha up here?" asked Carol.

"I'm keeping fit jogging and Sasha is getting her exercise too. Nobody minds – it's an unofficial extra patrol. We'll run past the fence so we can check it out. Come on, Sasha!"

Boobie gave them a brief wave as she jogged off. Sasha did not follow at first, but snuffled around the bush. However when Bobbie called her again she bounded after her mistress. They were soon out of sight.

"Well," said Carol, "there's the fence. We were right. This must be how the fence-cutter was getting in and out without being seen."

Raj took some snaps of the view and of the hidden entrance.

"Let's get back to the others now. I'd love to see a genuine secret passage inside a house."

Raveena trailed Melody and Iain, her head down as she unravelled her ball of string, leaving her trail for the others to follow. She was soon proved to have had real foresight, for the passage opened into a squarish space. A small space but with several passages leading off in different directions. They took one at random but this led to a cellar room full of junk.

"Just look at that pile of rubbish," said Raveena. "It looks like it's been there for a hundred years."

"I think some of it has," said Melody. "Well, this is a dead end. Let's go back."

As they returned, Iain shone his torch on the ground ahead of them.

"We *are* a bunch of donkeys!" he declared. "Look – there are our footprints in the dust. We should have known the way we want to go is where someone has left footprints."

"We don't know for sure the burglar used these passages," said Melody.

She did not sound too convinced and indeed they all were pretty sure the burglar *had* used the secret passages. So it proved, for at the next passage they tried, Iain shone his torch longways along the ground and they saw.

"Footprints! I was right. Look, I'm sure they're

the same size as the ones we photographed the night of the break-in."

"You're right," said Melody. "They're not clear but they look the same size and shape – like someone wore big boots."

She took a quick snap of the prints with her mobile's camera.

"You can see the prints show someone coming and going," said Raveena. "They point both ways."

"You know," said Iain. "If there's enough dust they might lead us to where the burglar actually got into the house."

"We're in the house already."

"He means, into where people actually live in the house," said Melody. "Maybe through a secret panel or hidden door or something and into one of the rooms or corridors."

They followed the marks in the dust – the footprints were often smudged and overtrodden – until they reached another division. This time however, one of the paths led to a flight of stairs. Or perhaps *set of steps* was a better description, for it was hardly proper stairs: they were made of old wood, blackened with age and the steps were narrow and warped. It seemed to go up and up a long way.

"Wow!" said Iain. "We must be in a sub-sub-basement if we have to go up all that way to get right into the house."

The whole structure creaked as they climbed

upwards and the children began to wonder if it was safe. They had reached the halfway point by then and it seemed as dangerous to go back as go onwards. Iain led the way, stepping very gingerly on each step.

"How on earth did a big man come up here without breaking something?" asked Melody.

"Maybe his weight caused these steps to become so dodgy," said Iain. "Though they must have been pretty rickety to begin with."

Raveena was silent. She had to concentrate like anything to lay down her string trail, while carefully watching where she put her feet. She didn't see then, though she heard the tremendous crack, as the step snapped beneath Iain's foot and he went plunging downwards.

SEVENTEEN

UNEXPECTED GUESTS

Iain had seen that the step ahead of him was missing, and he tried to skip over it. But the step he had all his weight on gave way with him off-balance. He fell through the gap, yelling out in surprise and shock. His

flailing arms caught part of the step above him and he hung suspended, arms shoulders and head all that could be seen of him. The step he was holding began to break too, and he slipped further down. Melody stood frozen for a moment, oblivious to the squeals of Raveena behind her. Then, at the very last moment, as it looked like Iain would plummet downwards and break a leg or worse, she dropped her torch and moved. She grabbed his arms just before he disappeared completely from sight. Raveena clambered forward to help but she shouted back at her.

"Stay where you are, Ravee! The weight of the three of us might break another step."

Melody felt awful. Iain could be seriously injured, yet she could feel him slipping from her grasp. What made it worse was it was dark, both of them having dropped their torches. They lay far below, shining into blackness and leaving them with only a feeble reflection of light they could barely see by.

"I'll get help," said Raveena, and she ran back down, careless of meeting with an accident herself. She had only been running a few moments, following her own trail, when she was suddenly blinded by the light of torches. She shrieked in terror.

"Calm down, Ravee," said her brother. "It's only us coming back."

She flung herself on him and gave him the kind of hug she'd not given him since they were really little kids. He pulled her arms away from him.

"What's happened? Has there been an accident?"

"Hurry! Hurry! Iain needs help – he's fallen through the stairs."

Raj and Carol couldn't understand what she meant, but they could see her genuine panic so they ran forward. They understood quickly enough when they saw the rickety old wooden frame that supported the steps – and a frantic Melody hanging onto Iain who dangled from a gap near the top. Iain felt a horrible mixture of fear and helplessness. He couldn't try to grab the step above him unless Melody released his arms, but she daren't do that. Her grip was the only thing preventing him from falling to the ground and suffering a serious injury. They saw that the others had arrived by the beams of their torches which lit them up as if they were on stage.

"Careful!" Melody called out anxiously. "These steps are dangerous. One of you climb past me if you can, but try not to put your whole weight on the steps."

Raj reacted quicker than Carol. He climbed carefully but with some haste, stepping on the sides of steps where they were firmer and with fingers digging into cracks in the wall for support. Carol followed but stepped carefully behind Raj so they were never both on the same step together. Raj stretched his legs to his utmost to straddle the missing steps, then knelt down to grab one of Iain's wrists. Carol, from a step below Melody, stretched herself out – gripping the crude balustrade to steady herself – and managed to get hold of part of Iain's arm.

"Come on!" she said. "Pull! Pull!"

Pull they did, and slowly and steadily, though a little awkwardly, they managed to raise Iain until he could lift his leg and get a foot on the upper step. Raj climbed up and away from him so that he could put his weight on the step he'd been on. They all let out a sigh of relief and Raveena, from below, clapped her hands in delight.

Iain shivered a little as he looked back at the shattered steps where he'd had such a narrow escape. Raveena had joined the others, with the aid of a hand up from Carol over the dangerous gap. She had the dropped torches and her ball of string in her arms.

"I don't fancy going back down these steps," she said. "It's not safe."

"We shouldn't have to," said Carol. "There must be a way into the house proper from these passages."

Raj beamed his torch along the new passage.

"See the footprints in the dust? Let's follow them."

It was very strange walking through the dim tunnel-like passage in such a large group. They felt squashed and a little claustrophobic as if they were in some deep, underground dungeon. They had torches, but as it was difficult to even go two at a time, the torches at the back threw off shadows from the children in front adding to the eeriness of the place. Not that there was much to see: the passage was dirty and musty and seemed to go on and on without break. At last however they came to a short flight of steps – stone steps this time.

"We must be in the house proper now," said Iain. "Look, this is newer brickwork."

Climbing the stairs, they found themselves in passages where they really could only go in single file. They were also brick-walled but neater and with narrow, wooden columns embedded in the brick every so often. These passages were shorter and bent at sharp right angles into other paths.

"You can tell we're well into the house," said Melody. "The passage is following the shapes of rooms now."

"If we could only find an entrance," said Raj. "It must have more than one way in and out of it."

"We ought to have come across something by now," said Carol, "but we've not seen anything like an entrance to the house proper."

"Well," said Raveena, "it's a *secret* passage so the ways in and out will be hidden – to keep them secret. I hope we find one soon, though."

She looked down at her ball of string, which was looking quite small now, then at the trail of string stretching back along the passage. She had no torch but the other children's torches were flashing this way and that so she could see well enough. She gave a little squeal.

"Oh, for goodness' sake! Look!" she cried; and she pointed.

They turned and saw clearly, in the light of four torches, that a wooden column protruded slightly from the wall. They had seen it before and not given it any attention but now they saw its other side. A long metal rod ran down it and attached to the rod was a small lever.

"You've done it, Ravee!" cried Carol.

She patted her friend's back then pushed past her and pulled at the lever with all her strength. For a moment nothing happened, so she pulled again. There was a slight grinding sound as if old gears were catching badly. Then there was a loud *clunk* and a section of the wall moved slightly inwards. They were all tremendously excited now and they pushed and shoved against the section with all their might. All at once the wall moved away from them and they tumbled onto a thick carpet. They raised hands to eyes, for the sun shone through long windows in a far corner, momentarily blinding them. A voice spoke loudly and sharply.

"My goodness! Margaret, I think you had better get more tea and cakes. We have some unexpected guests."

They looked up and saw a beautifully furnished room. Lady Agnes – the Laird's sister – was sitting in an armchair. She had grey hair tied in a bun and wore a pale blue dress and blouse. Despite her rather old-fangled appearance and stiff posture she did not seem *really* old and there was a twinkle in her eye when she spoke.

"Please bring those rugs by the fireplace and sit on them. They are somewhat worn so it won't matter if the dirt comes off on them."

They had not been in Lady Agnes's room before and were impressed by its large size and luxurious furnishings. They were also very impressed by Lady Agnes. Few people would be so nonchalant if a bunch of children burst out of a secret panel into their room. Not only was she not shocked or annoyed, she was treating them like invited guests.

"Awesome!" said Raveena, looking round the room. "It's like something out of *Antiques Roadshow*: this stuff must be worth a fortune."

Lady Agnes let a little smile flash across her face but pretended not to hear this.

"Come, children, sit round this table... ah, here's Margaret. Yes, and I believe the guests *I was expecting* have also arrived."

Margaret came in, pushing a trolley. Behind her came three figures.

"Howling hyenas!" yelled Iain. "It's Kirsty. And Calum and Davy. What are *you* doing here?"

Kirsty froze in the doorway. Her eyes bulged wide and her mouth gaped.

"*Gu dé an truaighe...*!" she sputtered. Davy laughed.

"Not a calamity, exactly," said Lady Agnes. "Just some surprising children."

Margaret set out a delicious tea, with scones, cakes and biscuits.

"Help yourselves; I will talk while you eat."

Lady Agnes waited, smiling, while the children grabbed cakes and biscuits and settled down to making them disappear as quickly as possible. Kirsty and her companions hardly ate anything but stared, astonished, at the opening in the wall. Lady Agnes nodded towards it and Davy and Calum went over to push it shut.

"I have not been back very long," said Lady Agnes, "but I've already heard something of your adventures. I've also discovered that the Laird has blamed the WFF for the trouble we're having here. My foolish brother has got hold of the wrong end of the stick as usual. That is why I invited David here."

"And Kirsty stuck her nose in, as usual," said Iain.

Kirsty glared at her brother.

"Now, now, behave," said Lady Agnes. "Children, I heard you have been supporting the WFF. Good! We should be working *with* them instead of blaming them for the sabotage." A smile wrinkled her face. "It seems that you have been exploring our secret passages. How on earth did you find your way into them?"

Despite mouthfuls of cake and sometimes talking all at once, the children managed to tell her about the clues they found at the manor and finding the secret passage. Lady Agnes gave no sign of surprise or concern about the children's investigations, not even when she heard of Iain's narrow escape on the broken steps. (Though Kirsty looked shocked). She merely complimented Melody and the others on their quick reactions. Davy however got quite excited.

"Those footprints you described can't belong to anyone in the WFF and the secret passages show how the real culprit was getting in and out. That's proof we're innocent."

"Not absolutely," said Lady Agnes, "but I'd say it makes a good case in your favour. Not that I ever thought you guilty. I know you all too well to ever think such a thing."

Iain noticed that Kirsty blushed, remembering her earlier rudeness about Lady Agnes. He grinned at her. Their host brought out a little leather purse. She drew out a white business card and peered at it.

"Oh, where are my glasses?!"

"Let me," said Raj, springing up. He took the card. On it was printed *Detective Sergeant Innes* and underneath in small print was a telephone number and email address. Raj examined it.

"ds.dinnnes@ardriaghpolice.scot," he read. "I see. He left this when he was here last time?"

"Yes. I will contact the sergeant and tell him what you have found out and *that* should stop the accusations against the WFF. I'll also ask my brother to see that the secret entrance you found is guarded."

"But what about the other bur—" began Raveena. Carol interrupted her.

"Yes, what about the burglary in the manor? That's probably the same person who cut the fences, isn't it?"

"Of course it is," said Davy. "You lot better get cleaned up now. Lady Agnes won't want your grubby fingerprints all over her good furniture."

"You'll want my grubby photos of the footprints we found," said Raj. "I'll get copies and leave them with Lady Agnes before we go."

"Give them to David," said Lady Agnes. "It is only right that the WFF hand in the evidence. I will telephone the sergeant to guarantee its authenticity."

"Add the photos I took of the prints in the secret passage," said Melody, handing him her mobile.

They charged out, leaving Davy to discuss a WFF peace treaty with Lady Agnes.

Once they were out of sight and hearing, they slowed down so they could talk.

"Why did you stop me telling about the other burglaries?" complained Raveena.

"Because until Harry is in the clear," said Carol, "we don't want anyone to know everything *we* know."

"Especially my sister," said Iain. "She'd be bound to blab."

"Anything we give away could lead back to Harry," said Carol. "We'll give Davy the evidence that clears the WFF, but keep the stuff about the jewel thieves back for now. It's a pity, because we won't get credit but it's for the best."

"What's up, Raj?" asked Melody. "You look like the cat that swallowed the canary."

"Lady Agnes just gave us a better way to get our evidence to the police quickly, without them knowing where it came from or it getting lost or ignored."

"How?" Carol's tone was disbelieving.

"By email of course. It was on the card she showed us."

"Do the police pay attention to emails?" asked Iain. "My dad's always complaining that folk in his office put off looking at them if they're busy."

"It's a personal address – anything we send will go straight to the detective investigating our burglary, not to their admin staff. If we posted our evidence, it would take a day or two to get to them and it might sit on someone's desk for ages before it was looked at. An email will be read right away – more or less."

"But they'll know who it's from."

"You can download stuff that lets you hide your computer location. I can create a new email address, too, just to send the evidence and they won't know who or where it came from."

"Wow!" said Carol. "You're a real super geek. If we act quickly, we can send the evidence to the police this evening."

They washed and changed into clean clothes in double-quick time and rushed back downstairs. Raj handed over photos of the footprints and the secret passage to Davy. He had also scrawled a quick description of the man the children had seen running in the grounds.

"You might have told us all this before," said Kirsty.

"It's fine," said Davy, laughing. "They wanted to explore their secret passage first. We'd have done the same at their age."

Lady Agnes stood up and signalled the children to wait.

"Before you go – our summer festival takes place in Ardriagh tomorrow. There will be a fete, stalls, fairground rides and musicians."

"I forgot all about that," said Iain. "I usually go with my family."

"Mr Wales has arranged for the film crew to be involved in some events. I believe he is doing it as a gesture of goodwill."

"I bet Oswald is thinking about the free publicity he can get," said Carol with a laugh.

They discovered soon after that they had been recruited to take part in Oswald's events. They did not mind, as the festival sounded like fun and they had taken their investigations as far as they could for the moment.

"One thing still bothers me," said Melody. "How will we get the necklace back to its owner without anyone knowing we got it from Harry?"

"We'll think about it later," said Carol. "The main thing is Harry doesn't have it now."

"We ought to visit him tomorrow when we get a break and let him know what we've done."

They decided to leave it like that. Later that evening Raj arranged their evidence files and emailed them to Detective Innes.

"Well, that's that," he told the others when it was done. "I know we've done good work but it's a pity we couldn't have been involved in the actual arrests. We'll miss out on the real excitement."

But he was mistaken.

EIGHTEEN

SHADOWING THE SUSPECT

Breakfast was a rather subdued affair. No one spoke about the burglaries or the evidence which Raj had emailed anonymously to the detective. The children put it out of their minds and went into town to prepare for the festival. They set off early; they wanted to visit the shops before it all started. Ardriagh was already very busy: there were hordes milling around, while people set up booths and performance areas for the singers, jugglers and dancers who would appear later. Even their shopping, limited as it was, took longer than expected because the town was so busy.

"That was murder!" exclaimed Melody. "But at least we've got a card and a present for Harry."

"And a card and some chocolates for Lady Agnes," said Raveena. "Are we late for our event?"

They made their way quickly to the area that had been reserved for the film people. As they arrived they saw a large blue truck draw up quite close to them.

"What is that doing there?" asked Melody.

"That's the Big Screen Bus," Iain told her. "Ardriagh is too wee to have a cinema so this comes sometimes. I suppose we call it a bus because it sounds friendlier; it goes round Highland towns and villages showing movies."

"This is the first time we've seen it. Does it not come round often?"

"Not in the summer, but we see it quite a lot in winter. It doesn't usually park here though."

"They must be going to show a preview of the film we're making," said Carol. "Yikes! Look what's happening now."

The truck engine started up again and a peculiar thing happened. The sides of the truck trailer began to push outward. The children watched, fascinated, for several minutes until the trailer had expanded into a broad, low-roofed cabin.

"I can see how it makes a cinema now," said Melody. "Though it's quite a small one."

"And here come the steps," said Iain. "They'll go to that door at the side where the customers will go in."

"I expect it will be free today," said Carol, "if it's to advertise our film."

Just then some Landrovers drew up in the parking lot. There was no surprise this time for they brought actors like Ronnie, Martin, Ravi and Susie, and crew like Liz and Rosie the dressers, Paula from make-up and Joe the props man. They could see too that the vehicles were packed with stuff in the back.

"That'll be costumes and props that they're going to show," said Melody. "I wish we didn't have to get made up. I'd rather wander around and see everything."

Melody and Iain were to demonstrate costumes and make-up and Carol was to take part in interviews along with the adult stars – something she relished.

"Besides," she said, "I can stand in for you, Mel, as well as answering for myself. All I have to do is put on a whiny voice and they'll think I'm you."

Melody swung a punch at her sister but she dodged away.

They went up and greeted their colleagues, though conversation was very brief as the adult film stars soon attracted a small crowd. Martin announced that they were going to have a question-and-answer session soon.

"When it's over, you can take pictures and we'll sign autographs. There will be a preview of our new film in the mobile cinema over there."

The crowd dispersed to watch the other events that were going on, although a few still hung around to watch the film people making their preparations. The children were roped into helping, carrying boxes and bags from the Landrovers. At last, when it was all ready, there was quite a crowd around them, pointing and chattering and taking photographs.

"Right, kids," said Martin, "your work's not over yet. You come with me to the interviews, Carol. The rest of you go with Liz and her team for make-up and costume."

A local radio presenter was going to ask the questions – some taken from the audience, some from reporters. They would be recorded and broadcast on radio and TV. Oswald would certainly get all the publicity he could have hoped for. Liz took her group of children to the two booths that had been set up for the make-up and props demonstrations.

"Now, Melody and Iain will demonstrate some of the fantasy costumes. Shhh! Be quiet, Raveena – we'll dress you up as an elf child, ears and all. Melody, Raveena: come with me and we'll look out some dresses for you."

While Liz was busy with the girls, Iain and Raj wandered over to the booth where Joe had laid out all sorts of props for show. He was sorry to hear that Harry had had a relapse, though they told him his friend was expected to recover. He got the boys to help him finish setting up his display. Meanwhile, quite a large crowd had gathered to admire Melody and Raveena who looked glamourous in silken dresses. Raveena was really enjoying all the attention. Paula sat them in chairs and announced:

"Ladies and gentlemen, gather round and view a miracle. See these horrible infants transformed into beautiful elf children before your very eyes!"

This brought laughter from the audience and brief glares from the two girls. *Horrible infants* indeed!

"I'm thirsty," said Iain. "I'm off for a drink. You want one too, Raj?"

"Get me a fresh orange and bacon crisps. I'll stay and annoy Raveena."

Iain found that as he pushed through the crowd, people were patting him on the back, grabbing and shaking his hand and asking him to sign autograph books.

"Thank you, thank you," he repeated, getting redder in the face with each book he signed, and more than once got the reply, "No – thank *you*!"

On his way back a few minutes later, he happened to glance up the street. He took a sharp intake of breath. Standing at the bus stop, waiting for the northward bus, was the Weasel.

Why was he leaving town when there was a big event here he should report on?

The Weasel had changed clothes and was now wearing a dark, greenish anorak, old jeans and a woollen hat. He was dressed for the countryside, including new boots. A rush of different thoughts flashed through Iain's mind. Was the reporter heading to the manor? Perhaps he was going to meet somebody. Iain and his friends suspected he might be involved with the burglary at the manor. Perhaps he was paying the burglar to steal stuff for him – personal stuff he could use for a story.

Melody, Raj and Raveena were surprised to see Iain pushing his way through the crowd towards them, clearly in a desperate hurry. In a breathless voice, he explained what was up.

"I want to follow him, but he might recognise me."

"We'll disguise you," said Melody, pushing him onto a chair. She rummaged in a box and brought out a bright, red wig.

"Don't be daft," said Iain. "Everyone will stare at me if I wear that thing."

Paula, thinking this was some game the children were playing, laughed and came over.

"Here," she said, "try this one."

She handed over a wig made of light, mousey-coloured hair.

Melody looked at it with disgust but placed it on Iain's head anyway.

"That's better," said Iain, looking in the mirror Paula held up for him. "It looks ordinary… but it doesn't look right."

"Your eyebrows are too dark. Wait a minute."

Paula searched and quickly found something that looked like a thick pencil. She ran this over his eyebrows and examined him.

"Not bad," she said. "It almost matches the wig exactly. Luckily your eyes are more grey than anything. They go with the wig colour quite well."

"Try these," said Raj – and he stuck a pair of thick-framed spectacles on Iain's nose.

"What!?" Iain moved to take them off, then stopped. "Oh! They're just plain glass. I can see fine through them."

"They make you look quite different."

"Good. That's enough – too much will be a nuisance, in fact it would probably draw attention to me."

"One last thing," said Paula.

Iain looked up, meaning to say he didn't need anything else, but he saw she was holding thin, transparent tape. She used this to make sure the wig was held in place. Then she combed the wig to hide the tape and the little bits of his own hair that were still showing.

"It's not very windy but you never know," she said. "No one will recognise you now."

"Be careful, Iain," said Raj, when Paula left with Raveena to finish her make-up. "If you spot he's up to something, find one of the adults at the manor – don't do anything yourself. I'll fill in for you here."

Iain stood up and suddenly realised people had been watching him being made up. They thought it was part of the demonstration and gave a brief round of applause, though Iain could hardly see how his simple disguise merited it. (Simple as it was, it did make him look quite different).

Iain sneaked out the back way and ran across the parking area. He knew a shortcut and it was just as well, for the last person in the queue was boarding the bus as he got there. He got on and paid his fare – he paid more than usual for although he thought the reporter was going to the manor, he might be going past it. Perhaps to the part of the glen where Oswald often had the film crew working.

The bus was much busier than usual and the only seat he could get was just in front of the reporter. Iain was relieved that the man paid no attention to him. For a mile or so the road from town was lined with trees and the shade they cast let Iain see the Weasel's reflection in his window. The reporter footled and fiddled and constantly checked his watch. He kept looking round the bus as if he was worried that he might be being watched. Then, to Iain's surprise and horror, he leaned over and spoke to him.

"Look, sonny, do you know how far it is to the bus stop near a red house?"

Iain was too taken aback to answer right away. A woman sitting opposite said,

"There's no red house on this road."

"There must be… it's called… uhm… it's called Tea Jerky. Or something like that."

The woman looked completely puzzled by this. So was Iain for a moment, then he suddenly realised what the reporter had tried to say.

"Oh, you mean *Taigh Dearg.*" Iain spoke with as strong an accent as he could in case his voice was recognised. "That's Gaelic – it means the Red House. It isn't actually red – I think it got that name because there was some murder there long ago. Red for blood, I suppose. It's one of the local legends."

"Of course," said the woman. "I remember now. Yes, it's quite a story." She looked as if she would like to tell the reporter the whole story there and then, but she looked up and said: "Here's my stop – the manor. Cheerio!"

"That's all very well but she still hasn't told me what stop to get off at. Do you know, sonny? You knew about the house name."

Iain groaned inwardly. He had meant to avoid being noticed and now he was having to talk to the man! But he realised that he had to make the best of a bad job. He turned his head – only slightly because he didn't want the man to get a clear look at him.

"It's two stops along. I'm getting off there myself. I'll let you know."

"Ta, son," said the reporter, then he sat back, ignoring Iain.

Iain wondered what to do next. Telling the man he was getting off at the same stop meant he would think nothing of Iain getting off with him. But what then? The stop at the Red House was a good bit past the manor but not close to anything else except a few scattered crofts. Why was the reporter going there? There was nothing for it but to play it by ear. He was sure the reporter was up to something and he must keep watch on him. The bus stop was approaching. Iain half turned to the man behind him.

"This is it now."

The reporter was so nervous, he tripped and fell over in his rush to get out of his seat. Iain helped him up and then led him to the front of the bus. Luckily, a man was waiting at the bus stop and signalled it to stop. Iain recognised the man and was almost about to say *hello* to him but caught himself just in time. He had forgotten for a moment that he was wearing a disguise. The man stared at Iain for a moment. Something about the boy was familiar.

"Come on – or get off," said the bus driver, impatiently. "I can't wait here all day!"

So he just shook his head, puzzled, and climbed on. Iain needed to get out of sight now. He crossed over and walked along a path until he was some distance from the road. Then he crept back and lay down among long grass and watched the reporter walking nervously up and down by the bus stop.

He was definitely waiting for someone.

Iain heard the roar of an engine and saw a moving cloud of dust. It was a man, riding a motorbike; he seemed vaguely familiar. Iain's heart fell. How would he be able to keep up with a motorbike? After the bother he had taken in disguising himself and his good work in dealing with the reporter on the bus too. It wasn't like detective stories where everything went like clockwork. Things kept going wrong. He watched while the motorbike slowed and rolled up beside the reporter.

"I can't ride on that thing – I'll fall off. Besides, you don't have a spare helmet."

The man laughed and patted his own headgear, which was an old rugby helmet – not a proper motorbike helmet. The man spoke with a strong local accent.

"Spare helmet? Never use them. Where I travel you don't see any cops. Now, get on. Glad to see you're wearing sensible shoes. We've a bit of a walk after I park this."

"Park? I thought you wanted me to get on."

"I do. We'll ride up to the old bothy and I'll hide it there. Then we've only a mile or so to walk down to the manor. Don't worry, it'll be safe and there's a something there you'll really want to see. Come on, man, get on!"

Iain suddenly realised he ought to get a photograph of the two men together. He had barely gotten his mobile out when the motorbike whizzed past him. He took a quick snap but when he looked at it, the bike was just a blur. He groaned as he watched them roar up the track.

"Now I've lost both of them," he muttered. "But I've still got one chance."

NINETEEN

DANGER IN THE TUNNEL

Iain ran onto the road and kept running. The bus going back to town was due any minute. He reached the stop just in time. He got off at the next stop which was closer to the manor. Then he walked back to where a stile let him climb over the wall that ran alongside the road. A narrow path soon joined a broader track. This led to the other side of the hill, where it bordered the manor grounds. The men were leaving the bike at the bothy. They would have to walk back down by quite a rough path – it would be hard going and slow them up. He wondered,

They're definitely involved in the trouble at the manor. Or at least, the motorcyclist is. The Weasel doesn't seem to be sure what's going on.

Iain quickened his pace. The Weasel's companion was a local who knew his way about the place. He would find his way down to the manor in no time, even if he *was* slowed up.

Some time later, Iain reached the point where the hill path came down to join the trail he was on. He looked up the hill but could not see anyone. Then he heard the whining, complaining voice of the Weasel.

"How far have we got to go now? My feet are killing me."

"Not too far, now." The other man laughed. "You should have bought your boots earlier and taken the time to wear them in properly."

Iain had already dropped to the ground and was hidden among long grass and heather. He located them by their voices, a little bit ahead of him. He waited until they were further ahead and then got up and followed them. He kept a little bit off the track so that he could dodge behind a bush if one of them should look back. However, neither did. They went straight on. The reporter walked awkwardly, his feet pinched by his new boots, which made it easy for Iain to keep up with them.

After a while, the men left the path into more rugged country strewn with rocks, bushes and more and more trees. The extra cover allowed Iain to get closer to his quarry. Soon they were entering one of the little woods that ran along the edge of the Laird's manor grounds. Iain wondered again what they were up to.

Why has he brought the Weasel here? He's a liability if he's going to be sneaking about the manor.

Iain got out his mobile and used its camera zoom feature like a kind of telescope, peering beyond his quarry at the wider grounds.

Where are the guards? There are supposed to be regular patrols. I can't see anyone.

Still, there was nothing to do but keep following them. However, he kept the mobile phone out and ready to use. If he could get a photograph of them in the manor grounds, it would show they were up to no good.

At last, they reached the end of the wood where it opened onto the manor grounds. Iain was puzzled.

What were the men up to? Were they going to the secret passage? They wouldn't know that it had been discovered. He hoped he hadn't followed them for nothing. They might just go away when they saw that everything was guarded now. Or was it? Where were the guards?

Iain let them get a little bit ahead of him now, for once they climbed into the manor grounds there would be less cover if he followed them. The men stopped at a low wall and looked around as if getting their bearings. Iain made up for his earlier thoughtlessness now. He raised his mobile camera and took several quick snaps, making sure one included the manor in the background. Now the men were over the wall and walking away from him. Iain jumped over the wall and ran quickly towards a little overgrown area. Just as he reached it, the Weasel glanced back. But Iain had thrown himself flat on the ground amongst tall grass, weeds and wildflowers.

Moving slower now, the men crept to the rear wall of one of the gardens and in through a narrow gate. Iain got up and ran forward when they were out of sight. He waited at the gate, his back against the wall, listening hard for any sound the men were making. He peered in. Nobody was there. He crossed through the garden – it was full of flowers and flowering bushes which filled the air in the enclosed garden with a delightful scent – and as he went, he realised now where he was. This garden was maybe thirty metres or so down from the Ladywell garden.

They were definitely going to the secret passage! Wouldn't they get a shock when they saw it guarded!

Iain rushed to the gate on the opposite side and peered through just in time to see the men creep into the Ladywell garden. He ran over and leaned back against the hedge beside the entrance. Just then he heard a *clack* as if two stones had been knocked together, followed by a loud, scraping noise. He moved round slowly and slinked through the entrance, moving cautiously along the inner hedge so not to be spotted. He peered round the next corner, and now he had a surprise. The secret passage entrance was open but it wasn't guarded. No one else was there but the Weasel. *What had happened? Where were the guards? Where was the motorcyclist?*

Iain found out the next moment as his arms were grabbed from behind and twisted up his back. A harsh, menacing voice rang in his ear.

"You little brat! Didn't think I spotted you trailing us, did you? Not that I blame you with that idiot with me." He twisted Iain's arm even more, so that he cried out in pain. "I've been a poacher and deerstalker too long to be fooled by the likes of you."

Iain managed to twist his head round to see his captor's face. He was shocked.

"Jack Soutar! But you were in jail!"

"How does he know you?" asked the Weasel.

"Didn't you know? I'm a local celebrity. The Laird had me prosecuted and the WFF gave evidence against me – just for poaching."

"You used dynamite and killed half the fish in the loch!" said Iain. "Then you shot a gamekeeper."

Soutar laughed as if Iain had paid him a great compliment.

"I only shot him in the backside – he couldn't sit down for a month. Anyway, I got out of prison early for good behaviour. I know how to bide my time. Now I'm getting my own back on him and his friends."

He pushed Iain forward. Seeing him close, the Weasel almost jumped out of his skin.

"That's the boy on the bus! He was sitting in front of me. Damn it! He even told me where to get off the bus."

Soutar relaxed his grip on Iain slightly, threw his head back and laughed so loudly Iain wondered why nobody came running to see what it was about.

"Hah! I knew you were an idiot but I never thought you were as big an idiot as that." He twisted Iain's arm again. "Now, laddie, why were you following this little weed?"

"Aargh!" Iain thought frantically, then had an inspiration. "I… I've always wanted to be a reporter. I knew he was one of the big town reporters staying in Ardriagh. Ouch! When I saw him leaving when all the others were at the festival I thought he must have a scoop. I thought I could find out what his big story was all about."

The Weasel looked rather pleased to hear this – he really believed Iain's story. Soutar just laughed.

"A likely story – mind you, it's maybe a better one than our friend there ever wrote in his paper. But it doesn't matter. I can't leave you to tell what you've seen – so you're coming with us."

He pushed Iain towards the secret passage.

"There," he said to the Weasel. "It's really something isn't it? I heard tales about this when I was a bairn. Now few even know the tales; but we know it's true now. Come on, let's get on with it. Follow me, I know the way."

"Is it safe?"

"Aye, Danny boy, it's fine. I've been in a couple of times now and it's in good nick, though it took me a while to figure where everything went. In you get!"

He pushed Iain forward so hard that he nearly fell on the slippery steps. Dan Wissall (the Weasel) bent low and moved cagily after Soutar into the underground tunnel. The three of them moved down into the darkness. As they neared the bottom, Soutar produced a small torch from his pocket and switched it on. The light flickered somewhat at first, but he shook it and a steadier beam shone out, albeit not particularly bright. They walked on, Iain's arm aching as his captor kept it twisted up his back. Soon they reached the chamber-like area Iain and his friends had explored before. A solitary candle sat on a bit of rock and beside it stood another man. Soutar shoved Iain towards him.

"Keep a grip of this brat, Mike, while I get my stuff."

Soutar began to examine one of the old underground walls. Suddenly he knelt, laying his torch on the ground.

"Here it is." He grunted and dug with his fingers into the earthen floor. "Up you come!"

"What's all this about?" The Weasel's voice was puzzled – and anxious. "I thought you had a story for me."

"You mean about the burglary here? And the other burglaries?"

The Weasel looked very nervous now. He began to back away from Soutar. But before he'd moved a few steps, Soutar leapt up at him and knocked him down with one punch. The reporter lay on the ground, groaning. Mike chuckled – he loosened his grip slightly, but Iain didn't try to escape. He was curious to find out what this was all about. Soutar kicked the reporter.

"Give him one for me too," said Mike.

"Why are you doing this?" Iain's voice was high and strained, showing his fear.

"Nosy Parker here," said Soutar, "has been sniffing around asking questions he shouldn't. About burglaries no one's supposed to know about."

So that was it! thought Iain. *Soutar was the local man telling the burglars which houses to rob. And the Weasel had been investigating the same robberies as Iain and his friends! They had really been mistaken about him.*

"He must have recognised me or Pete," said Mike, "and knew we'd done time for stealing jewels."

"I've never seen you before," the reporter whined.

Mike laughed and pulled at the hair on his head. It came off – it was a wig.

Iain gasped and the reporter gasped too. It was Baldy – he had worn the wig and shaved off his beard so no one would recognise him. Iain's spirits dropped even further.

"You know me now," Mike said. "I nearly got caught by the police thanks to you. They picked Pete up this morning. I only got away because I was in town at the time. Jack here had seen the cops arrest him and warned me. Brought me here to wait for you."

"But I haven't told the police anything *yet*…" The Weasel's voice died out as he realised what he had said.

"So you *were* going to rat on us – only someone else ratted first. I bet it was Harry. I wish I'd thumped him harder."

Soutar finished his digging and pulled up a thin wooden slab, which covered a hole.

"What have you got there?" asked Mike.

Soutar pulled out a tool box and opened it. "Look!" He raised a long, powerful-looking wire cutter.

"You're the one who released the animals," said Iain.

"Man! Who else?" He put the cutters down. "Most of them are away at the Ardriagh festival and the Laird's put half the guards off duty – he thinks I've been frightened off by the dogs no doubt. Well, we'll give him a big surprise – and something worse."

Now Soutar took out a couple of plastic bottles filled with some liquid.

"This'll warm the old buzzard up." He laughed – a nasty laugh.

"Th-that's not petrol in those bottles, is it?" The Weasel was still dazed.

"No." Again the nasty laugh. "It's something much better for starting a fire."

"You can't mean to burn the manor down!" Iain was horrified, too horrified to move. So too it seemed was Baldy, though he managed to say,

"Wait – someone could get killed. I'm a thief, not a murderer."

"Och, nobody will get killed. It'll only be a wee fire, nothing too serious – just enough to make a good mess o' the place."

However, Iain caught a gleam in Soutar's eye and saw the expression on his face. The man didn't really care how bad the fire was or who got harmed. Soutar brought out thick twine from his pocket and tied the Weasel's hands. He meant to tie them both up and leave them here – with the fire. Even if they weren't near it, smoke could get at them and choke them. The boy looked frantically around. The torch had been switched off and the candle's weak light made everything further than few metres away invisibly dark.

"Hurry up and let's get out of here."

Baldy Mike sounded nervous. He seemed to be afraid of Soutar, so afraid that he would go along with setting fire to the manor – leaving two people tied up and at risk of their lives. This made Iain feel very afraid for he had seen Baldy attack Harry. What kind of man was Soutar if a thug like that was frightened of him?

"Calm down. I'll just finish tying this guy's legs and then I'll do the boy."

Just then, Iain saw that the reporter was staring away from them at something beyond the light of the candle. Unable to use his hands, he nodded in the direction of the nearest tunnel.

"L-l-look! W-what's that?"

Iain turned and Soutar stopped, with the Weasel's legs half tied, and also turned. A deep growling sound echoed in the chamber and a pair of shining eyes glowed in the darkness. Iain stared, for a moment dumbfounded. He could see the faint outline of a powerful animal. Then he caught a flash of white and he realised what he was seeing. He shouted out, terror in his voice.

"Wolf! It's the escaped wolf – the one that hasn't been caught yet!"

"He's right!" The Weasel's voice almost squeaked, he was so frightened. "Free us, for heaven's sake."

Soutar bent down slowly and picked up his torch. He shone its feeble light at the creature and saw powerful shoulders, bared canine teeth, thick fur. It growled louder now, more fiercely, and began to advance. It looked ready to pounce on them at any moment. The Weasel looked as if he was about to faint. It was too much even for Soutar.

"Back away slowly," he said. "It'll go for us if we run."

"What about the boy? If we leave him it will savage him."

"Mike, lad, for once you've had a good idea."

236

Soutar gave a grim laugh and grabbed Iain. Then he pushed him towards the beast. Iain couldn't keep his balance and fell in front of it. It loomed over him, sniffing, then it straddled him, its powerful head coming down on his face.

"The wolf's got him!" The Weasel's voice was a screech. "It'll tear his throat out."

"Why don't you offer it your own throat instead."

Soutar disappeared into the darkness, followed by Baldy Mike. He might not be keen on helping with murder, but he wasn't going to risk himself to stop it.

TWENTY

CHASED BY THE WOLF

The crowds were thinning a little but the festival was still going strong. The film stars' interviews were over but some reporters hung around photographing or filming the other events. Melody and Raveena, fully costumed and made up, were signing autographs (much to Raveena's delight some people assumed she was a minor star). Even Raj had been 'elfed up' as he called it and was standing watching proceedings with elf ears and a dashing cloak over his shoulders. Being more of a bystander than anything, he was the first to spot Calum and Kirsty pushing their way through the crowd towards them. Kirsty laughed when she saw them costumed and made up. Raj looked embarrassed but his sister looked annoyed. She thought she looked wonderful and that they ought to be admiring her. Melody merely shrugged her shoulders.

Carol joined them at that moment and looked round.

"Where's Iain? Is he not part of this?"

"Oh," said Melody. "He saw something he wanted to check up on."

Her friends exchanged guilty glances. Should they tell?

"You're hiding something," said Kirsty with a glare. "What's my daft brother up to now?"

"Sizzling sausages!" said Carol. "If Iain is doing something risky, Kirsty has a right to know. So do I."

"Know what?" Kirsty looked worried. "Come on! Spill it."

"Iain saw the Weasel heading out of town," said Raj, "and followed him to see what he was up to."

"Who on earth is the Weasel?" asked Calum.

"He's a reporter. We thought he might be buying stuff from whoever burgled the manor," said Raj.

"You know, to get diaries and letters to use for a story."

"I never liked the Weasel," said Melody, "but I'm sure he's not dangerous."

Calum slapped the top of his head.

"We've just come from the police station," he said. "We went with Davy to show the proof that we are innocent. They'd arrested a man they suspected of burgling houses round here. He was too small to be our burglar, but he had a partner – a much bigger man – who escaped. He's the one who put your friend Harry in hospital, so Iain could be in real trouble if *he's* the man that burgled the manor too."

The children had not thought the jewel thieves were the ones causing trouble at the manor, but they couldn't be sure. What if Baldy was the one the Weasel was going to meet? Iain could really be in danger – and he was, though not from the person they thought.

"He's in disguise!" exclaimed Raveena. "No one will recognise him."

"It doesn't matter what he looks like – if he's caught he'll be in real trouble."

The children looked at each other doubtfully. Melody and Raj felt miserable. They wondered now if they should have ever let Iain go off on his own, even in disguise.

"We've got to catch Iain," said Kirsty, "and bring him back."

"Too late!" said Raj. "He's been gone ages."

"Where will he be by now?"

"There's only one place to look," said Carol. "The manor. If he's not there or near there, we'll never find him."

"Damn!" exclaimed Kirsty. "Davy's still at the police station. We can't wait for him to drive us back."

Calum looked round and saw the Landrovers parked nearby. He grinned.

"Come on!" he said.

He was speaking to Kirsty but the rest followed him and he was in too much of a hurry to tell them to stay put. He passed one Landrover, glimpsing in as he went and at the next, stuck his head in the open window.

"This one – they've left the key."

He started the engine, not waiting for the others who piled in as he backed out of the car park. Kirsty was in front and the rest in the back. A few minutes later they were roaring up the road towards the manor.

"Isn't this illegal?" said Carol. "After all, you don't have a driving license."

"I've got a provisional license," said Calum. "Anyway, it doesn't matter. We've got find Iain before anything happens to him."

"If anything *has* happened to that silly brother of mine, I'll kill whoever's responsible."

The children at the back exchanged glances at this odd mixture of anger mixed with worry for her brother. Since he was already breaking the law in taking the Landrover, Calum ignored the speed limit and shot up the road at a tremendous rate. It hardly seemed any time at all before they were roaring through the main gates of the manor. At that very moment Iain was lying prone in the underground chamber with a huge beast hulking over him.

Iain felt along the thick fur and found what he wanted – the collar!

"Get off me, Sasha, you big wet hairy beast!"

He pushed the guard dog away from him and wiped his face. Sasha had been licking his face for she recognised him even in disguise. Dogs are not fooled that way. It was all he could do to keep her off him while he freed the Weasel from the knots tying him. The reporter was so astonished he couldn't say a word. Iain held the candle up to his face, wondering if he had fainted with fright. He hadn't but he was trembling all over. Sasha nudged Iain and he put the candle down so he could hug her.

"It's lucky for me you turned up – but you've known about the tunnels all along, haven't you? Bobbie's let you run free and you smelled strangers in the tunnel and came after them."

The Weasel had recovered just enough to ask what was going on.

"I knew it was Sasha by her white paw but I

pretended she was the wolf and they fell for it. You snarled beautifully, didn't you, Sasha?"

Iain was wittering on out of pure relief, for he had truly been in fear of his life. Now he calmed down and thought what to do next. He stood up, took out his phone to use its torch feature and, holding Sasha by the collar, followed in the direction that the two men had fled. Sasha might not really be a wolf but she was a strong, trained guard dog and with her at his side he could hunt them down. As he set off, the reporter tried to get up to follow but he hadn't properly recovered from the blows Soutar had given him. He sat down almost at once, groaning. All he could do was look at Iain and the dog disappearing into the tunnel.

Bobbie wrung her hands with frustration. She peered back the way she had come and shouted to her fellow guard, Ricky.

"Can you see her?"

"No, she's not around here. It's your own fault, you know. You shouldn't let her off the leash like that."

"She's never run off like that before – she just seemed to disappear. What's that?"

"Don't know – sounds like someone banging on a door, but it can't be."

Curiosity – and the fact that even off-duty they were still security guards – drew them towards the sound. It came from the edge of the manor grounds where they bordered a wood. As they got nearer to the sound, they noticed an odd, raised hump of ground, partly obscured by small bushes. All at once, this seemed to burst open and a thickset man shot out, stumbling towards them. A second man staggered out shortly after, ran a few metres, then tripped over a stone and fell on his face.

"What the devil!" cried Ricky. He moved to take hold of the larger man. "Soutar! Jack Soutar! What have you been up to?"

His reply was a back-handed blow to the guard's face. Bobbie grabbed Soutar's other arm and they struggled for a moment before he managed to push her away. He gave the still-stunned Ricky another blow and kicked him as he fell. Just then, Iain appeared, holding Sasha's collar, just as Bobbie was grappling with him again.

"Get him, Sasha!" he cried.

It didn't matter that it was the wrong command. Sasha could see her mistress being attacked and she almost pulled one of Iain's fingers out as she broke away from him. Soutar barely saw the dog before it leapt on him, knocking him over. Then she had a grip on his wrist which he couldn't break free from, despite a few kicks at her. Iain ran up, holding out the twine that Soutar had tied the reporter up with.

"Here, use this. Get his hands behind his back."

That wasn't easy to do with Sasha attached to one arm, but Ricky tied one wrist then pulled it round and tied it to the other arm just above Sasha's muzzle.

Baldy Mike was on his feet now and running. Suddenly he turned and ran in a different direction – and tripped up again. He was on his feet quickly but a gang of children appeared running towards them, with Calum out in front. Mike barely ran twenty metres when the teenager brought him down with a flying rugby tackle. Mike was bigger than Calum but moments later he found himself sat on by Kirsty and four other children.

"What's been going on here?" demanded Bobbie, pulling Sasha away from the prisoner. "How did you all pop out of the ground? Wait a minute, it's Iain, isn't it?"

Iain grinned broadly and pulled off the wig which Sasha had nuzzled loose.

"There's a secret passage down there. It takes you into the manor and another branch comes out near the zoo fence."

"Ah!" said Ricky. "That's the way of it. We can guess what this pair have been up to then."

"Yes, the evidence is back down there." He turned to his friends. "It's a good thing you all turned up. Mike might have got away."

"Not with Sasha around he wouldn't," said Bobbie as she tied Mike's hands. "Still, you were all a big help."

Just then a very dazed Weasel staggered out from the tunnel, astonished to see the crooks were now sullen prisoners. He followed the guards back to the manor with their captives. The children went with them, Sasha leaping around them, nuzzling hands. They explained as they went along how they had discovered the secret passage – and Iain described how he had been captured and how Soutar had intended to start a fire. The Weasel took notes furiously as they talked.

"Sasha saved the day though," said Iain. "They thought she was the escaped wolf and ran for it – she helped us find the passage in the first place you know."

"Of course she did," said Bobbie, bursting with pride for her dog. "She's a real heroine."

The prisoners were taken into the manor and locked in an old storeroom until the police could come and arrest them. Ricky and another guard went to search the secret passage while Bobbie and Iain explained to the Laird what had happened. Kirsty was about to give Iain a piece of her mind for taking such risks, but she was interrupted by a voice from above.

"And when the men return from the underground passage with the evidence you will see what a complete ass you have been, Ronald MacKay!"

They all turned to see Lady Agnes coming down the stairs, dressed in a tweed outfit. The Laird's cheeks glowed a bright red, he stuttered and harrumphed, but at last with a rather sheepish expression he said,

"Well, *harrumph*, I suppose I may owe certain people an apology."

"Suppose!? You silly goose! I told you that the police were being presented with evidence about who was breaking in and cutting the zoo fence. I didn't say they had been arrested yet – but you cancelled the extra patrols, making it easy for these scoundrels to break in again."

"Well it all worked out for the best," said Iain. "If Soutar had seen extra security he probably wouldn't have broken in and wouldn't have been captured."

The Laird gave Iain a weak but grateful smile. His sister shook her head and *tsk-tsked*. It was only then they noticed Melody behind Lady Agnes; she had sneaked upstairs for some reason. They were too excited to think more of it.

There was a sudden uproar and Davy's sister, Morag, strode into the hall.

"Those idiot guards at the gate won't let us bring our Landrover through."

The Laird was too astonished and embarrassed to speak. Lady Agnes however found the situation amusing.

"Why do you need to bring it up here?"

"Not here," said Morag. "We were taking the wolf to the lodge where you have medical facilities for looking after sick animals – but we have to get through your zoo's gate first. Billy's out in the Landrover keeping an eye on it."

"The wolf?" The Laird was suddenly alert. "You've caught the escaped wolf?"

"Not so much caught as found," said Morag. "Some crofter's shot her, when she went for a sheep, and she's been wandering around wounded."

"Come with me – by the way I owe you all an apology, but I'd rather make it to all of you together and in full public view. I'll speak to the guards and get you through to the lodge immediately."

He strode out and Morag (with an astonished look on her face) followed.

"Now, children," said Lady Agnes, "everything is settled nicely here. Come with me and I'll drive you to Ardriagh. We will tell the police what has happened here, after which all our worries should be over."

TWENTY-ONE

END OF ADVENTURE

This time Lady Agnes drove the Landrover so that Calum would not get into trouble. He sat in the front squeezed beside Kirsty, which suited them both. The journey to town seemed to take an age compared to the last time they had sped up this road. Of course, Lady Agnes felt no need to break the speed limit this time. In town, the festival was winding down now but there were still plenty of people milling about, clogging up the streets.

"Look," said Calum, "we'll be quicker walking. Let's get out here."

"Very well. I'll park this vehicle somewhere – wait for me outside the police station."

They tumbled out and waved goodbye to Lady

Agnes – though they expected to see her again soon. They moved off and pushed their way through a milling throng. Pointing fingers and amused faces reminded Melody, Raj and his sister that they were still wearing costumes.

"I wish I'd got rid of all this," Raj said, "before we left the manor."

"I don't!" Raveena waved at the folk staring at her. "Oh, someone's coming out of the police station now."

The crowd had thinned a little so they could see PC Cowan bring out a man in handcuffs – Snubby! He led him down the steps with Detective Sergeant Innes close behind.

"What's going on?" said Iain. "Where are they taking him?"

They stood stock still in surprise. Then Carol struck her palm with her fist.

"You know – I bet they're taking him to the hospital. I bet that crook has claimed Harry was involved in their robberies."

"But why not just send someone to arrest Harry?" asked Melody.

"Because he's in hospital, you donkey." Carol grinned smugly at her sister. "They won't let him out till he has recovered, so the police have to go to him."

"We'd better hurry after them," said Iain, "and see what's going on."

They did hurry. They barged their way down to the hospital and rushed past reception, ignoring the shouts of attendants and nurses.

"Well, Mr Puddock, what do you say to these accusations?"

Sergeant Innes' voice was quiet and even but there was an edge to it which said, wordlessly, *you had better have a good answer or you are in serious trouble.*

Before Harry could answer, clattering footsteps made everyone look round as a troupe of children (and two teenagers) entered the ward. Snubby stared at them, puzzled for a moment, then suddenly recognised them.

"Those brats again! Little so-and-sos!" (He used another word, not 'so-and-sos').

PC Cowan gave him a dig in the ribs.

"Ow! Police brutality. Did anyone see that?"

All the children at once cried, "No!"

Snubby was so angered by this he completely lost his temper and made a dash at the children. Calum tackled him, bringing him up short. Kirsty, the boys and Carol joined in, grappling with the crook. Finally, Melody joined in, though all she seemed to do was grab a bit of his jacket. It turned into a rather ridiculous-looking brawl with some children being knocked back and leaping on him again. At last, the policemen got hold of him.

"That won't go down well in court," said Sergeant

Innes, "when we give evidence that you tried to attack these witnesses."

"They don't know nothin' about our caper."

"They are witnesses to your attack on this man here."

"That was an accident. They didn't see right. We just had a bit of an argy-bargy about a job he was doin' for us and he slipped. We gave him a necklace to fix up for us. Only he sold us out, so I'm givin' him up too."

The children looked at each other, puzzled at this interpretation of what they knew. Iain guessed first and whispered to his friends,

"He doesn't know it was our evidence that got him caught – he thinks Harry gave him up."

Sergeant Innes smiled to himself. He knew it wasn't Harry for, confined to his hospital bed, he could not have gathered the evidence that had been passed on to him. He did not know though that it was the children who had provided it. He did suspect though that Harry might have been involved in some way.

"Well, Mr Puddock," he said, "what do you say to that?"

Harry frowned and furrowed his brow – he was thinking hard.

"Some of it's true, but a lot of it's lies."

"It ain't lies!" Snubby bawled. "He's got the necklace. Make 'im show it. He can't have got rid of it stuck here in hospital."

Harry looked a little downcast, then he slowly reached for the drawer of his bedside locker and brought out the little jewellery case. Melody gave a sharp intake of breath and put her fingertips to her lips.

"See! I told you he had it." Snubby was positively gloating. "Open it and show them."

The detective took the case, examined it with great interest – then opened it.

"What have we here? Yes, definitely a necklace. Not a very good one though. It could do with a bit of repair."

It was Melody's necklace, much smaller than the one they had switched. There was room for one of Melody's brooches and a ring as well. She tried hard to stifle a giggle. Snubby stood staring, open-mouthed and gasping like a fish on dry land. Harry was equally surprised but had the sense not to say anything. He gave Melody a sly, grateful glance however. Sergeant Innes, a broad smile on his face, held the open case under Snubby's nose.

"Are these the stolen jewels you say you gave to Mr Puddock?"

Snubby looked confused and puzzled. He was silent. Melody spoke up now.

"I gave these jewels to Harry to fix for me. You can see they're a bit damaged." She had a sudden inspiration. "Why don't you ask the nurse? She'll know what possessions Harry had when he came in.

She would have had to put them all away while he was being treated."

"I'll do that. Meanwhile I'll just check the locker. Let's see." He bent down and rummaged about for a couple of minutes. "Ah! Nothing here. Anything under your pillow, Harry? No? Maybe we'll check under your mattress."

"I have a better idea," said Melody. "Sergeant – have you searched your prisoner yet?"

"No, miss. We found stolen goods in his caravan, so we didn't bother because we had so much evidence. He's just been questioned so far, not charged."

He nodded to PC Cowan who held Snubby tight, while the Sergeant searched his pockets.

"Here's something," he said, and pulled out a necklace, shining with diamonds, emeralds and rubies. "Whew! She's a beauty – worth twice the rest of the other stuff put together."

"This is a frame-up!" Snubby was angry, but at the same time there was defeat in his eyes. "One of you cops slipped it in my pocket."

"Why would we do that, Mr Gosse? We have plenty of evidence against you without the necklace. It's nice though that we'll be able to return it to its owner. Take him away."

Snubby – or Peter Gosse as they now had to think of him – was led away. He gave the children a hate-filled glare but said nothing. It was all over with him.

As he was led through the door, Raj said under his breath,

"*He'd have gotten away with it if wasn't for us pesky kids.*"

"And the WFF," added Carol, "and don't forget Sasha – and Lady Agnes."

"No," said Sergeant Innes, who was finding it hard to keep a straight face. "By all means, don't forget any of them." He looked down at Harry who looked very relieved. "You are a lucky man, Mr Puddock, to have friends who would go so much out of their way to help you."

"He certainly is," said a voice. They all turned to see the Weasel standing in the doorway. "By the way, Sergeant, when you get back you might see new prisoners arriving. Thanks to the children here, the crook who escaped your net has been caught, as well as Jack Soutar—"

"Soutar? That villain! So he was the local crook helping the jewel thieves."

"Yes, and he was behind the manor burglary and fence cutting. I've got a great story, unfortunately—"

"Unfortunately, what?"

The Weasel grinned a nervous grin. "Unfortunately, I'll have to describe how the intrepid reporter was rescued from a terrible fate by a boy and his dog. Never mind, my editor will love it. I might even get front page."

In that moment the children decided he wasn't

really a Weasel but Dan Wissall, (not-quite) intrepid reporter. Melody stepped forward.

"Mr Wissall, we thought you were one of these reporters who stick their noses into people's private business and were rude to you. We were wrong – you were investigating the robberies too."

Sergeant Innes raised an eyebrow at the 'too' in her statement but merely said.

"Well, this all goes to show that when you get information about criminal activity, you should tell the police right away."

To their astonishment – and lasting pleasure – Sergeant Innes shook each of their hands.

"Well done, children. However, I hope you remember that you can get into trouble when dealing with dangerous criminals. The same goes for the investigators who provided us with the information about the jewel thieves. I hope you will warn *them* that they should wait until they're a bit older before they take on another case."

With that he made a loose kind of salute and, grinning widely, he handed Melody her jewel case and left the ward.

"Jumping giraffes!" exclaimed Carol. "He knows."

"I think he just guesses," said Iain. "He can't really know."

"He has a theory," said Raj, "which he hasn't enough evidence to prove."

"I don't think he will bother to try to find it," said

Dan Wissall. "He is pleased to have solved the case. Still, he'll have to put up with everyone knowing how you found the secret passage and practically caught two of the crooks by yourselves."

"You're going to tell everyone what we did?" asked Carol. "And put it in the newspapers?"

"That's my job, darling. Though I don't know everything for sure, there's more than enough for a great story. You all did great, especially Iain who got me out of a spot. However, I think the detective gave you good advice. Wait until you are a little older before you investigate any more mysteries."

They all promised they would and it was easy to do so, for, as Raj said later, *we'll all be a little older next week.* Next moment, Wissall had his mobile out and took several quick snaps of the children and Harry in his bed.

"That's all I need for now," he said. "But I'll want to interview you for a follow-up story later. This will be big!"

And with that he left, practically running down the corridor in his hurry to get his story to his newspaper.

"Well, I like that – not!" said Raj.

"Oh, forget about that," said Melody. "Let's see how Harry is."

She skipped over to the bed and put her arms round him. He blushed and pushed her away.

"He said one very true thing, that detective. I do have some very good friends. Here, give me that case, young lady. I'll fix your jewellery for you – better than new. Now, I'm a bit confused – and it's not just because of the bang on my head. How about you all tell me the whole story."

And they did, very eagerly as they'd had to keep a lot of it secret up until now. Raj was particularly proud about the part his helicopter had played in uncovering the thieves' hideout. When at last they came to the end, and their seeing Peter Gosse being marched into the hospital, he laughed then grinned at Melody.

"That was very neatly done by you, miss. Where did you learn the trick?"

To the children's surprise, Melody blushed slightly and smiled coyly.

"I know!" said Carol. "We did a show where we played urchins who pickpocket someone. We had to practise slipping stuff in and out of pockets to make it look good. Anyway, that wasn't really hard. We caused such a commotion fighting with Snubby he didn't notice a thing when she slipped it in."

"Would you believe it!" said Calum. "She reverse-pickpocketed him."

"It wasn't really dishonest," said Kirsty. "After all, he really did steal the necklace in the first place, so it was only fair it should be found on him."

Melody blushed but she soon forgot her embarrassment as they all congratulated and high-fived each other.

That was the end of adventures for the children that summer. There was still the movie, which was fun to be in or just watch being made, and enough free time to play and explore or just generally muck about. The story of the capture of the burglars at the manor was a sensation for a few days. Oswald Wales was very pleased with how things turned out as it made for great publicity for their film. However, as far as the folk at the manor were concerned it was quickly forgotten. The children sometimes talked about how they had helped catch the crooks, with the different parts they had played getting exaggerated in the retelling. Iain began writing it all down, trying to turn it into an exciting screenplay. Would they see themselves – or young actors playing themselves – on screen one day? Harry was soon back at work and, true to his word, he fixed Melody's necklace. Not only that, he made her a brand new one, a beautiful bracelet for Raveena and medallions for everyone, inscribed with the words, 'Incredible Investigators'. But what was wonderful was that one side of the medallion had the image of a dog. It was Sasha – and there was a sixth medallion just for her.

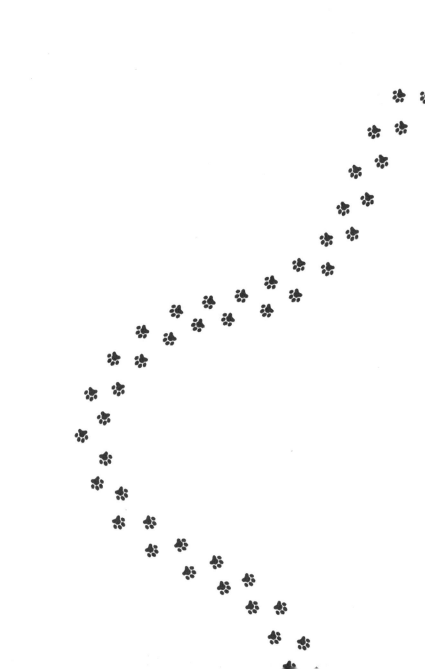